AMNESTY

A SHAWNEE ADVENTURE

also by

BOB GIEL

A CROW TO PLUCK

The Shawnee Series
SHAWNEE
SAVING THE TELL
STOLEN RIVER

AMNESTY

A SHAWNEE ADVENTURE

BOB GIEL

HAT CREEK

HAT CREEK

an imprint of
Roan & Weatherford Publishing Associates, LLC
Bentonville, Arkansas
www.roanweatherford.com

Library of Congress Cataloging-in-Publication Data
Names: Giel, Bob, author
Title: Amensty/Bob Giel | Shawnee #4
Description: First Edition | Bentonville: Hat Creek, 2025.
Identifiers: LCCN: 2025940569 | IBSN: 979-8-89299-056-1 (trade paperback) |
ISBN: 979-8-89299-057-8 (eBook)
Subjects: FICTION/Westerns | FICTION/Action & Adventure |
FICTION/Thrillers/Historical
LC record available at: https://lccn.loc.gov/2025940569

Hat Creek trade paperback edition June, 2025

Cover by Casey W. Cowan
Cover art by Frederic Remington (1861-1909)
A Post Office in Cow Country, Oil on canvas
Editing by George "Clay" Mitchell, Lisa Lindsey & Don Money
Interior Design by John Bredesen

For
James Grassi
&
Michael Lee

Prologue

New Mexico Territory
1880

THE SANTA FE RING, AN almost decade-old network of unscrupulous attorneys and corrupt government officials, determined to increase their fortunes at the hands of the citizens of New Mexico, tightened their grip on the governance and economy of the territory. They pirated old Mexican land grants, subdivided them, and sold them to unsuspecting settlers. Then they reacquired them through legal proceedings weighted in their favor, only to sell them again to others. Their riches and power grew.

Into this lawless society, General Lew Wallace, a battle-tested soldier of the Union Army and newly appointed governor, stepped resolutely. With the same determination he employed during the War Between the States, Wallace broke the back of the organization within a year of taking office. Many of its members were exposed as the charlatans they were. The ring's influence and resources were severely diminished.

However, Logan Yaeger, an attorney indirectly involved in the land swindle, escaped not only prosecution but identification. Forewarned, he absconded with much of his loot. But Yaeger was not ready to end his life of crime.

Going underground, he assembled a group of hardened criminals. Under his direction, they conducted raids on everything that presented ill-gotten profits. Their operations succeeded such that they threatened the very existence of the Wallace administration. Renewing his resolve to bring them to justice by whatever means possible, Governor Wallace embarked on a secret trip to Chicago.

1

RANDI SWAYZE DIRECTED HER HORSE along a narrow dirt trail. The view of the road told her she faced a steady upward climb that would ultimately bring her somewhere close to the top of the mountain. That point right now was out of her sight because the trail wound around the mountain's back end.

Randi was tall and well proportioned, maybe a little too well, but better that than skinny. Sitting straight and riding expertly, she was a progressive woman who disapproved of the side saddle prescribed for women of the time, electing to straddle a standard rig used by men. With a pleasant, oval face boasting fine features, her dark brown hair hung in large curls to her shoulders under a straight brimmed, light colored straw hat. Her white blouse and khaki split riding skirt were geared to weather the extreme heat of this mountainous Mexican terrain. She wore brown, high-heeled boots that were hot and uncomfortable, but she accepted that they were necessary.

What Randi would find at the end of this trail was anyone's guess. Her hope was to finally locate the object of her months long hunt, the elusive and reclusive Alonzo Pearce.

As she rode, her thoughts drifted back to Chicago and the start of this case. God, it must have been four months ago, as she recalled entering the office of her employer, the Pinkerton Detective Agency.

ALLAN PINKERTON SAT BEHIND A huge, paper-strewn desk. His abundant beard measured three inches below his chin. In contrast to the facial hair, his head was almost bald.

The room was well appointed in ornate decor with a leather couch on the side and matching chairs in front of the desk. The desk itself was mahogany with leather inserts held in place by silver headed tacks. Striped paper covered the walls. Several decorative coal oil lamps were mounted on the walls. A large window behind Pinkerton's desk bore the lettering, *The Pinkerton National Detective Agency*. It was readable from the street below.

Pinkerton looked up as Randi entered. "Good day, Miss Swayze," he said. His Scottish accent had abated over the many years since his immigration to the United States, but it was still noticeable. "You're right on time."

"Your message said it was urgent." She moved closer to the desk.

"The urgency is to get you started on this case. Please, sit down."

Randi sat facing the desk as Pinkerton gathered some paperwork and began to assemble it and place it in a folder.

"I had a visit from the territorial governor of New Mexico last week. He's asked the agency to find someone for him, unofficially."

"Unofficially?"

"And discreetly."

"This must be important for the governor to come all the way here instead of sending you a message."

"It is." As he spoke, he gestured with the folder in his hand. "And he stressed keeping this private. He even wanted to carry out our meeting secretly. New Mexico is faced with a serious outlaw problem, serious enough to threaten the safety of the territory as well as the security of the governor's administration. His fear is that he might be removed from office if he can't resolve this. His law enforcement authorities have so far been unable to get a line on the organization and the person behind it—"

"And you want me to find this individual?" There was both anticipation and hesitance in her voice.

"No, that's not it at all. The governor's best people have not been able to make a dent. He's decided to scrap the legal approach. He needs someone to infiltrate the gang and bring it down from the inside, no matter what it takes."

"Mister Pinkerton, I think you've got the wrong agent—"

"No, Miss Swayze, I've got exactly the right agent for the object of this case."

"I... guess I don't understand."

"Sorry. I'll explain. Since the governor has exhausted every legal avenue open to him to no avail, he's decided to use tactics outside the law. His chief territorial marshal has suggested using a known criminal to infiltrate the gang. That person is the one you are being assigned to find and bring in. His name is Alonzo Pearce. He's known to have used the alias, Shawnee. This is the file we've been able to pull together on him." Pinkerton handed the papers over to Randi.

She leaned forward and took the file, then she settled back to peruse the pages inside as Pinkerton continued.

"You are to track him down and convince him to meet with the governor. The payment for his services is amnesty which the governor has guaranteed. Once he agrees, you are to bring him to New Mexico and set up a secret meeting between him and the governor. That will be the end of your assignment. Interested?"

Randi leafed through the pages as Pinkerton finished. "Yes, of course," she said. "What is the timing for all this?"

"The governor considers this vitally important. It must be done thoroughly, but without delay. The governor's contact information is on the last page there. That must remain top secret."

Randi rose from her chair. "Then I'll start immediately. I do have one question. Why me?"

Pinkerton smiled, a knowing smile. "Precisely because you are a woman. You will be less threatening to the witnesses you'll need to interview to locate Pearce, and to Pearce himself. You've proven yourself to be one of my best agents. I have every confidence you'll be able to pull this off."

Randi smiled back. High praise from the man who not only ran the military intelligence operation during the war, but who single-handedly established the country's first national detective agency. The same man who chose to personally hire her. She was both flattered and apprehensive, but did not voice either, saying only, "Thank you."

"Best of luck," he said.

She closed the folder and left the office, already certain she would start in Shawnee, Kansas, Pearce's birthplace, and that her cover would be that of a newspaper reporter researching a story on Pearce. She expected this to be an intriguing exercise.

————————

RANDI'S SEARCH OF THE RECORDS of Shawnee revealed the birth of Alonzo Pearce to Seth and Isabel Pearce in 1847. Sketchy personal recollections of older citizens told of the hanging of Seth for his participation in the renegade organization known as both Quantrill's Raiders and Bushwhackers. Several of the accounts identified members of the Jayhawkers, a group of Northern supporters, as those responsible. Among

others, they named Carl Teverence, a feed and grain merchant, Otto Daylock, a hardware dealer, and a scout known only as Old Sam. No further
records existed regarding Alonzo, save one. The local newspaper files
recounted the murder of Carl Teverence, allegedly committed by Alonzo
Pearce. The story claimed that Alonzo dragged Teverence out of Shawnee to a spot a short distance from the town. When witnesses reached
the location, Teverence was found brutally assassinated, and Alonzo was
observed fleeing from the scene. There was also a handbill listing Alonzo
as the suspect and offering a reward of two hundred dollars.

Within those records, Randi found an additional wanted poster
issued on Alonzo, originating in Abilene, Kansas, for the attempted
murder of a hardware dealer named Otto Daylock.

Imagine that. Teverence, dead at Pearce's hand, Daylock, surviv-
ing an attack by Pearce. Certainly sounded like a vendetta. Her first
lead. Was it possible Daylock might still reside in Abilene?

Randi boarded the next stagecoach leaving Shawnee, heading for
Abilene. Still in the guise of a reporter for an Eastern newspaper, she
searched Abilene for the location of Otto Daylock's hardware business, hoping this lead would bear fruit.

Dressed in a pretty blue dress that accentuated her figure, she
stepped into the store and scanned the interior. A young man in a
white shirt with a starched collar and necktie approached her.

"Can I help you, ma'am?" he said in a high pitched, youthful voice.

"Yes, please. Is Mister Otto Daylock here?"

"Why, yes. He's in his office in the back." The young man flashed
a look of curiosity.

"May I speak with him, please?"

The young man hesitated for a second as if to bring to mind the
next question he should ask. Then he proceeded, "Can I tell him
who's...?" Oddly, he faltered there.

"Randi Swayze. I'm a reporter for the *Cincinnati Clarion.*"

His mouth opened, but no sound came out. Then, "A reporter? A newspaper reporter?" His voice raised an octave, betraying his astonishment.

Right, a lady reporter. Not his usual workday encounter. "Yes. I'm working on a story I think Mister Daylock can help me with." She stopped there to allow this all to sink in.

After a few seconds, his mouth closed.

"Would you please ask Mister Daylock if he would kindly see me?" she asked.

That seemed to give him impetus. He recovered and turned toward the rear of the store. "Yes, ma'am."

Randi looked around the store to pass the time it would probably take for the clerk to complete his task. Nicely appointed for a hardware store. Daylock must have been doing quite well to afford the well-constructed shelves and display cabinets exhibiting his wares.

The young man returned after a few seconds. "Mister Daylock said to send you in."

Randi smiled. "Thank you." She stepped past him and tapped on the door in the back. "Come in," a man's voice said. She stepped inside.

Otto Daylock was a big man. He sat behind a simple wood desk in this sparsely furnished office. A small window on the side wall did not allow enough daylight through it, necessitating a lighted coal oil lamp on the desk to facilitate the paperwork in which he was involved. His broad shoulders drooped noticeably, and his sizeable paunch caused him to sit far enough away from the desk to appear uncomfortable. With a puffiness that gave the impression of ill health, his round face included hanging jowls and tiny eyes. The dark hair was thinning and streaked with gray. He looked up as Randi approached.

"Good day, Miss... Swayze, is it?" His voice was deep and a bit foggy.

"Yes, that's right. I'm a reporter for the *Cincinnati Clarion.*" Randi stopped just shy of the desk.

Daylock studied her for a second. "So Amos tells me. He says you think I can help you with a story?"

"I'm doing a series on the lives of wanted outlaws in general, and, right now, one in particular, a man named Alonzo Pearce. In my research, I discovered you had a wanted poster issued on him, back around 1867, for attempted murder. May I speak with you about that incident?"

As she spoke, his face changed from curiosity to disquiet. That was recognition right there. He knew Pearce. She hoped she hadn't backed him into a corner.

Daylock leaned back in his chair. His gut and rounded shoulders limited his range of movement. He was quiet, thoughtful. "Why should I help you?" he asked.

Randi had to maintain her cover. She couldn't give away her real reason. "I'm an independent woman trying to be gainfully employed. Your assistance in bringing this story to the public would really help me to get ahead."

Daylock studied her for a long moment. "If I do, you got to keep my name out of it. I got a good business going here. I don't need that stuff drug back up to haunt me."

"I promise I'll do it anonymously."

A frown crossed his face. "Come again? Anona-what?"

"I'll keep your name out of it. I won't even mention your location or your business. You'll just be an eyewitness who prefers not to give his identity. Newspapers do that all the time."

His face relaxed some. "Well, since you put it that way, reckon it won't hurt none to tell you about it. What do you want to know?"

Well, that worked, thank God. The detective's tool of choice—lie to get at the truth.

Randi reached into her handbag and brought out a small notebook and a pencil. Instruments of both trades, investigator and reporter. "Let's start with some background. What brought the incident about?"

Daylock shrugged. "Hell if I know. This Pearce fellow walked into my store and just started pushing me around. So I pushed back. We got into it pretty good, as I recall, and he was just whipping me, him being younger and all. So I went behind the counter to get my gun. Figured that'd cool him off. When I come up ready to shoot him if he ain't leaving, he shot me. Got me right here." He indicated the spot in his side with a finger.

Randi grimaced as a way of showing empathy as he continued.

"Ain't been right since. Well, anyways, he runs out and leaves me there on the floor bleeding and all. Couple of my friends found me and got me to the doc. By that time, Pearce was long gone, I reckon. The marshal said he was going out after him, so I figured I'd sweeten the pot if you catch my drift. I had a wanted poster printed up and put a reward on it. I forget how much right off, but it got circulated around these parts pretty quick-like. Never done no good, though. Far as I know, nobody never cashed in on the reward."

"My, that was quite an experience. Tell me, how did you know Pearce? Did he live here?"

"Naw, he was a cowhand. Come to town with a herd of beeves got drove up from Texas. One of the first ones to make the trip, as I recollect."

"Then you didn't know him."

"Naw."

"I guess I'm confused a bit. If you didn't know him, how did you know what name to put on the handbill?"

"I, eh… I—"

She had to be careful not to box him in or he'd shut it down. "I don't mean to sound like I'm badgering you, Mister Daylock. Just call it reporter's curiosity. Please understand, your name will not be attached to this in any way. And, other than the few facts I'll use in my article, nothing you tell me will leave this room. But I'm quite curious how you came to know Pearce. Did you meet him in Shawnee?"

For whatever reason, Daylock pounced on that. "Yeah, that's it. I knew him in Shawnee. Yeah, when he was a kid. He come in here that day wanting me to remember him for some reason. When I didn't recall him right off, he got mad and started in on me. I was just defending myself, and he shot me with no call to."

Daylock was lying, that was certain. But, at least, he told most of it, no matter how twisted his version was. If she pressed him any further, he'd probably throw her out of here. One more question should do it and should change the mood. "Well, that certainly satisfies my curiosity. May I ask you one more question?"

Daylock harrumphed, but allowed it.

"Do you remember where that herd Pearce rode for came from?"

"I done told you, down Texas way."

"I mean was there a specific ranch or brand?"

Daylock thought for a moment. "Yeah, there was. I remember 'cause the town made such a big to-do about it being the first herd coming north like they was. It was a big T, the brand was. Stood for...." He hesitated while his mind reached back. "The Tell Ranch, that's it. The Tell Ranch."

Randi jotted that down and closed the notebook. "Thank you, Mister Daylock. This will help me immensely."

"Well, you're welcome, young lady. Now, just you remember, now, you can't use my name or where I'm from. You remember that."

Randi smiled. "Absolutely, sir. You have my word. And thank you again." She turned for the door.

"What you going to write about Pearce?"

She stopped but did not turn around. She couldn't let him see the smirk on her face. "Based on what I now know about him, probably that he's a hothead and a potential killer."

"Ain't no *potential* about it, I'm afraid. He's a sure enough killer. I guarantee you that."

Randi's smile broadened as she left the office.

2

I T WAS EARLY EVENING ON the same day of the Daylock interview. The hotel room Randi had rented was clean. The walls were painted a sky blue that was pleasant enough, but the place was not very comfortable. The bed was lumpy and the cloth appointed easy chair was anything but that. It was, however, only for the one night so it could be tolerated. Not the worst accommodations she had experienced.

She sat in that chair pouring over the notes she had made during her meeting with Daylock. Then she opened the file Pinkerton had provided her recounting people known to have had involvement with Alonzo Pearce. She pondered a dilemma. Which course would bear more fruit, a trip to Texas and the Tell Ranch or to Youngstown, Ohio to interview Dr. Foy Banning? If distance were a deciding factor, she was closer right now to Texas than to Ohio. However, for Randi, it was not a question of miles, it was her investigative curiosity that was driving her at this point.

The background information she learned about Pearce's early life in Shawnee, coupled with the impression she developed as Daylock related his tale, made her suspect that Pearce was not as bad as he was made out to be. She wanted to know more about Pearce and, in particular, about his character. Since the file indicated Banning's encounter with Pearce was a more recent experience, Ohio would be the next leg of her journey.

Decision made, Randi settled in for an uncomfortable night's sleep. She rose early to freshen up as best she could. At the depot of the Kansas Pacific Railroad, she was able to lay out the route that would ultimately bring her to Youngstown. The station agent estimated the duration of the entire journey at between one and a half and two weeks. This brought to mind Pinkerton's caution that this must be done thoroughly, but in a timely manner. Even though this move was backtracking, the interview was important for the insight it could provide into Pearce's character.

She boarded an eastbound train that morning. Soon after arriving in Youngstown, she located the office and residence of Foy Banning, MD. A cab brought her to the location just before the noon hour.

It was a well-maintained white, two-story home on a quiet residential street in the eastern section of the city. The wood shingle suspended from a short pole that jutted out from the porch eave identified the structure as Banning's office.

Randi stepped from the cab onto the sidewalk and told the driver to wait. Engaging another cab would be next to impossible in this quiet section of the city. She moved through the front gate and walked the short distance to the porch. The four steps brought her to the varnished wooden door with the glass panel in the center. She turned the key on the door frame that operated the doorbell. There was a fine lace curtain behind the glass. Definitely a woman's touch.

The door opened to reveal a slim, attractive woman in a simple dark green dress. She was about six inches shorter than Randi and appeared to be about the same age as Randi's twenty-seven years. Her light brown hair was pulled back tightly in a bun. She smiled and asked, "May I help you?" Her voice was light, but she spoke plainly.

Randi smiled back. "I'd like to see Doctor Banning if I may."

"Whom should I say is calling and what is your complaint?"

She thought Randi was a patient. "I don't actually have a complaint. I'd simply like to speak with the doctor. I don't have an appointment, but I'd be glad to wait."

"What is the nature of your business with the doctor?"

Well, she was persistent, Randi gave her that. "I'm a newspaper reporter. I believe Doctor Banning can help me with an article I'm writing."

"And your name?"

"Randi Swayze."

The woman extended her hand. "How do you do. I'm Prudence Banning. I'm Foy's wife as well as his nurse."

Randi shook hands with her. "Well, you are certainly thorough, Missus Banning."

Prudence chuckled. "Foy is between patients right now. I'll see if he can speak with you." She stepped aside to make room for Randi to pass. "Won't you come in?"

"Thank you." Randi went inside into a large room with several chairs placed close to a door on the side that was marked, Doctor's Office. The room was pleasantly decorated with paintings of outdoor scenes as well as several display cases containing items of cut crystal and fine china. On the other side of the room was a large archway that was blocked off with a heavy burgundy colored drape. This would be the way from the waiting room to the rest of the house.

Prudence tapped on the door to the office and entered, closing the door behind her. Randi wandered the room, taking in the decor. A few seconds later, Prudence emerged. "Foy will see you," she said matter-of-factly.

Randi stepped into the office as a tall, sandy haired man rose from his sitting position behind the desk situated toward the rear of the room. He wore a white laboratory coat under which was a starched collar, a white shirt, and a dark blue cravat.

"Good day, Miss Swayze," he said pleasantly. "I'm Doctor Banning. How can I help you?" As he spoke, he gestured toward one of the chairs that faced the desk.

Randi sat rather primly. "I'm working on a story I think you can help me with."

"Go on," he said. He retook his seat.

"I'm doing a series of articles on the lives of wanted outlaws. My research tells me you had an encounter with one about five years ago. I'd appreciate your telling me about it and about him."

Banning studied her closely. "Which outlaw are you referring to?"

"Alonzo Pearce, although you might know him as Shawnee." Randi produced her notebook and pencil and poised her hand to record.

"I know him as both. In my opinion, he shouldn't even be called an outlaw. I had much more than what you term an encounter with him. He not only saved my life, he helped me bring my father's murderer to justice."

"I see. Tell me, what was he like?"

"He was unlike anyone I ever met, before or since. He had a code he lived by. If he liked you, there was nothing he wouldn't do for you. He proved that several times over. He would not abide anyone mistreating a woman or ganging up on anyone. While his methods were perhaps questionable, his morals were rooted in basic Christian values. If you ask me, there should be more men like him. The world would be a much better place."

Randi spent a few seconds writing his words in her notes. "My research tended to indicate that, but this not only confirms it, it illustrates it. Have you been in touch with him since the incident?"

"No. Shawnee is not the type to write letters. You must be aware of the price on his head. That tends to keep him on the move and out of touch."

"Yes, I know. I just wish—"

"That you could locate him?"

"Well...."

"Miss Swayze, I would not help you do that even if I could. I have no interest in causing Shawnee difficulty. I'm sure he has enough of that in his life already." There was a trace of scolding in his voice.

"Doctor Banning, I assure you—"

He leaned forward in his chair. "You're not a reporter at all, are you?" His voice now was accusatory.

Damn. Randi sat frozen, then tried to recover. "No, Doctor Banning, you're right. I'm not a reporter. I'm an investigator for the Pinkerton Detective Agency." As she spoke, she produced her identification wallet and opened it for him to see. "We've been asked to locate Mister Pearce, but not to cause him the difficulty you might assume."

She needed to make this right before he threw her out of here.

"But to cause him difficulty all the same, right? I'm afraid I'm going to have to ask you to leave now, Miss Swayze. I don't wish to discuss this any further."

Randi leaned forward. "Dr. Banning, please let me explain."

"How do I know this is not some kind of trick?"

"You don't. All you have is my word that, while my methods were misleading, what I say is true. Please...."

Banning pondered that. He reached into his vest pocket and drew out his timepiece. "You have two minutes," he said as he opened the watch face.

She had to talk fast. "It is true that I'm trying to locate Pearce, but not to arrest him. I'm actually trying to help him. He's been given the opportunity for amnesty. I want to find him to make him aware of that offer."

"Amnesty? Who would offer that?" Banning continued to monitor his timepiece.

"I can't tell you that. But the offer is genuine. It comes from a trusted source. The difficulty involved is that Pearce would have to do something quite dangerous in order to earn the amnesty. I can't tell you what that is either. What I can tell you is, when I find him, and I will find him, it will only be to make the offer. If he refuses, I'll walk away, and I won't divulge his whereabouts. I promise you that."

"The promise of a liar?"

"Disguises are a device detectives use at times to facilitate an investigation. But I swear to you, I am not lying about this. I mean Pearce no harm at all. I'm simply tasked with delivering a message."

Banning let out a heavy breath. He closed the watch and put it away. "I don't know why, but I believe you."

Randi sat back. Whew!

"That does not preclude the fact that I can't help you. As I said, I've had no contact with Shawnee since I last saw him, it must be five years ago. I wouldn't begin to know where to look."

"Well, thank you at least for your time," Randi said as she closed her notebook. "And for believing me as well as your insight into Mister Pearce. That will help me when I speak with him."

Banning thought for a moment. "I do know someone who might have had more recent contact with him. But she's all the way out in Colorado."

Randi perked up. "That's not a problem. Who is this person?" She reopened the notebook.

"Her name is Amelia Scocroft. After my mother died, she raised me until I was eight. She was involved in the incident, and she got to know Shawnee pretty well. Let's just say they were close for a time. She told me that, when he left Bodeen, he actually doubled back to say goodbye to her. She hasn't mentioned him in any of her letters, but it is possible she's been in touch with him since he left. Long way to go if I'm wrong though."

"But worth it if you're right," Randi said as she finished writing.

"She should be easy enough to find. She runs a boarding house in Bodeen. I called her Meelee. That was how I mangled her name when I was a kid. Tell her that. It should put her at ease talking with you."

Randi rose and put her notebook away. "Thank you again. And again, I apologize for the deception. By the way, how did you see through it?"

"Simple. You never mentioned which paper you write for, and you weren't aggressive enough in your questioning. Any reporters I've come in contact with use the prestige of the paper they write for, and they almost badger you to get what they want."

Randi flashed a smile. "I'll keep that in mind. Goodbye, Doctor."

"Good luck, Miss Swayze. You're going to need it to find him. Most of all, be honest with him."

3

RANDI'S TRIP TO COLORADO, PRIMARILY by railroad, consumed another two-week period, landing her in Denver at dusk. After a quick meal at a nearby cafe, she sent a telegram to Pinkerton headquarters apprising her employer of her progress to date. Because of the lateness of the hour, she did not wait for a reply. She determined that Bodeen was reachable by coach, and one left at midnight. Wanting to lose no more time, she immediately booked passage and then tried to make herself comfortable in the stagecoach depot's waiting room until boarding time. No relaxation was achieved.

Mulling over the more than a month she already invested in this case, she was disappointed in the lack of developments. This Scocroft woman would have to have a worthwhile lead or it was on to Texas and the Tell Ranch. Another possible wild goose chase. Was she missing something? She never expected this lack of even a trace of this man, but, then again, he'd been successfully eluding the law for almost fifteen years, longer than most fugitives stayed alive. Was he going to magically appear because Randi Swayze was on the case? Not hardly. She had to keep digging and not worry about being Pinkerton's first female detective to fail. Not yet.

Randi spent about four hours in that wooden, bench-like seat trying in vain to sleep. The hard, unforgiving nature of the chair, coupled with her inability to shut her mind off, made that next to impossible. Then, about ten minutes before boarding time, she dozed, only to be awakened by the station agent's call, "Stage is leaving."

She roused and quickly grabbed her large carpetbag, forcing herself to haul it outside to the waiting coach. After handing the driver her bag, she entered the conveyance to find herself the only passenger. Not even the possibility of a conversation. Well, maybe this would be more conducive to sleep. At least, the seats were cushioned, well, sort of.

The driver's loud call to the team split the quiet night air as the coach lurched forward with creaks and squawks. The noise and unstable nature of the carriage negated any possibility of rest. She saw herself conducting her interview through bleary eyes.

The sixty odd miles of rough trail between Denver and Bodeen were just as bouncy as the beginning of the trip. Randi was constantly pitched from side to side as the coach rocked across uneven roads. That, coupled with the driver's periodic shouts at the team to keep up the pace, not only prevented sleep, but jolted her out of each attempt to rest.

Just after dawn, the coach roared into the main street of Bodeen and came to a stop at the depot. Randi stepped down to the ground and readjusted her clothing. She was disheveled from being pitched around inside the carriage. The only saving grace of this trip was the fact that the driver courteously handed her luggage to her while apologizing for the rough ride. She thanked him and requested the location of Amelia Scocroft's boarding house. He complied and provided directions which she followed gratefully.

Her eyes were blinded temporarily as the sun rose during her walk to the boarding house. She shaded her eyes with her free hand. The house was on the east end of the town on a small tract of land, perhaps a little less than a half-acre. A large, white frame house of two stories, it had a screened in porch that reached around both corners of the front of the house. Probably for sitting in the evening, without the constant annoyance of bugs. An enclosed stable was situated to the rear of the structure. It disappeared from her view as Randi approached the house. She mounted the three steps to a screen door that allowed access to the porch. Beyond that, she crossed the porch to the dark green front door as the screen door slapped shut, the action of an attached spring. She knocked.

A few seconds passed before the door opened. In front of Randi was a slim, blonde woman in a floral print dress covered by a food stained full apron. She was only half a head shorter than Randi and had bright blue eyes with a penetrating quality. Her long hair was piled and held in place with combs. There were fine age lines around her eyes and mouth. Her smile seemed genuine. "Good morning," she said. Her voice seemed to smile as well.

"Good morning," Randi said. "Amelia Scocroft?"

"Yes. Did you want a room?"

"That was not my original intention, but maybe I should. My name is Randi Swayze. I'm an operative for the Pinkerton Detective Agency." No more deception. Be truthful to get the truth. "I've actually come to talk with you, but my trip has been so tiring that I probably should take a room and rest."

As Randi spoke, the woman's smile changed to puzzlement. "I see," she said tentatively.

No, she *didn't* see. "I'm sorry. I should explain."

"Yes. Why don't you come in?"

Randi stepped into a parlor furnished tastefully, but modestly, with upholstered chairs and a matching couch placed around the room. A large bookcase containing many volumes, varied in size, the titles of which were not readily visible, stood against the back wall. She faced Amelia as the woman turned from closing the door. It was time to get into it. "First, I should tell you I was advised by Doctor Foy Banning to seek you out."

Surprise crossed Amelia's face. "You know Foy?"

"Yes, I spoke with him recently. He said he used to call you Meelee. He said that was how he mangled your name when he was a boy."

Amelia's mouth opened slightly. "Yes, that's right. How…how is he?"

"He seems quite well."

Randi observed uncertainty and uneasiness in her as Amelia gestured to a nearby chair.

"Please, sit down." There was interest—as well as a little suspicion—in the other woman's voice.

"Thank you." Randi set her bag down and sat on the edge of the chair. Amelia took the chair next to her and sat, leaning toward Randi.

"As I said, I'm a Pinkerton agent." As she spoke, Randi pulled the wallet from her handbag and displayed the badge and identification card within. "Our agency has been tasked with locating Alonzo Pearce. I was hoping you might be able to help me."

"I… no, I can't."

Randi raised a calming hand to address Amelia's alarm. "Please, hear me out. I'm not looking to arrest him. Actually, just the opposite. I've been authorized to offer him a chance for amnesty, but I have to find him first."

"Why should I believe you? I've been questioned by the law before. They tried to trick me into revealing his location."

Randi leaned forward. "Miss Scocroft, I'm not the law. Pinkerton is a private agency. There's a lot I can't tell you about this, but the truth is, Mister Pearce has been identified as being uniquely qualified to do something that could result in full amnesty for him. That is my only interest in him."

"That all might be true, but it doesn't change the fact that, even though I wish I did, I don't know his exact location. The last I heard from him at all was a letter he sent me last year, pretty much out of the blue."

Last year? That was more recent than anything she'd gotten so far. "Do you still have the letter?" Randi's voice raised an octave in anticipation.

"Yes, I do."

"May I see it?"

Amelia showed resistance. "I'm not in the habit of sharing my personal items with strangers, Miss Swayze, even if they do represent authority."

"I have no authority, Miss Scocroft. I can't stress that enough. The only thing I plan to do is deliver the message to Mister Pearce. It is strictly his decision what he does. If you have any feelings for him at all, and I believe you do, please help me help him. Maybe that letter will give me a clue that will help me find him. Please let me read it."

Amelia pondered the request silently. "All right, I'll get it." She rose and went to the staircase on the side of the room that led to the second floor. As she ascended the steps, Randi sat back into her chair and looked more carefully around the room. Obviously decorated for the calm and comfort of the guests. She wondered where Meelee relaxed. As she gazed, a light-headedness came over her, just slightly, but enough to make her aware that the effects of sleep and food deprivation were at work. She needed to address that soon.

In a few minutes, Amelia returned with a rather dog-eared envelope. She handed it to Randi.

No return address. Postmarked Crimshaw, New Mexico, July

28, 1879. Addressed to Amelia Scocroft, c/o General Delivery, Bodeen, Colorado.

Randi temporarily forgot the weakness she had just experienced
as she reached out the letter inside and opened it carefully. It was as
worn as the envelope. Obviously, she'd read this many times. Banning
having said they were close just took on new meaning. Randi read
through the letter.

> *Dear Amelia,*
>
> *I hope this finds you well. I am writing you to tell you that
> I am safe so you do not worry about me. I know it is a long
> time that I have not wrote to you. I did not want to get you
> mixed up in my life again because I care about you too much
> to do that. My only reason for writing to you now is to tell
> you that I am going to Mexico so as to stop running. I helped
> out a lawman here and now he is helping to get me across
> the border. I just want you to know that I will be fine. I hope
> you are fine too.*
>
> *Love,*
> *Lon*

Interesting. Randi glanced up from the letter. "So do you think he's
still down in Mexico?"

Amelia shook her head. "I don't know. I hope he is. He'd be safer
there than here, but I don't know."

Randi folded the paper and placed it carefully back in the envelope. She handed it back to Amelia. "The truth is," Randi said. "Knowing what I now know about him, I hope he is too."

Later that evening, Randi was watching the sun paint the sky as it
said goodnight. She heard Amelia come up behind her.

"You're already in love with him, aren't you?"

Randi spun around.

"That's absurd, I never even *met* Alonzo."

"Who said I was talking about Alonzo?" A smirk spread across Amelia's lips. Randi turned back around.

"It's a beautiful evening, isn't it?" Amelia's voice was almost a whisper.

"Well, I suppose it is."

"Randi, can you fall in love with a sunset?"

Randi turned back around. "Are you feeling okay, Ms. Scocroft?"

Amelia giggled. "I'm fine, but you didn't answer my question."

"Well... I... you could love a sunset, but it wouldn't be like being *in* love with one."

"That's what it's like to love Alonzo. You could love him, but he isn't going to love you back the way you want to be loved."

Randi drew her arms close and wrapped them around her own body, but there was no chill in the air.

"Are you going to Mexico?"

Randi hesitated, gave her a thoughtful look. "I don't want to get ahead of myself, but I'm definitely going to Crimshaw. In fact, I should start right away."

Amelia placed a hand on Randi's arm. "I'm not trying to delay you, but you *do* appear a bit weary. By the time your horse is ready, it's gonna be dark. I'm sure Crimshaw will be there no matter when you go. I have a comfortable bed with clean sheets on it upstairs, and I'm a pretty good cook. Perhaps you should rest before you go on."

A slow smile spread across Randi's face. "You're absolutely right. I will, thank you."

ANOTHER TWO WEEK JOURNEY SOUTH across Colorado and

New Mexico using a number of different stagecoach lines put Randi close to the southwestern-most tip of the New Mexico Territory, about thirty miles north of Crimshaw at a U. S. Army post known as Fort Craig. An active military installation, the fort was surrounded by a ten foot high log wall. Once inside, Randi learned that the final leg of her trip had to be made on horseback because no public transportation went farther south.

Finding herself running low on funds, Randi sent a wire to Pinkerton headquarters requesting more operating cash and to file an account of her progress. A short time later, Pinkerton wired the money and a favorable reaction to the report. The substantial amount of the advance required cashing by the post paymaster.

With her finances replenished, Randi attempted to hire a horse and riding rig to continue her trip, only to be told that rentals were restricted to within a confining area around the fort. Anything further than that required the purchase of the animal and tack. Not in a position to protest or bargain, she paid the fifty dollar price and chose a young bay with white stockings and requested a standard saddle. She had no intention of making this expedition into wild country on an uncomfortable sidesaddle.

Her next purchase was the range clothing necessary for the ride, and .38 Long Colt ammunition. From her carpetbag, she fetched a holster and a nickel-plated Colt Lightning revolver. She inserted the holster onto her skirt belt and loaded, then seated, the gun. After placing her dress in the carpetbag, she lashed the bag to the saddle and began her journey.

At the outset, she could not shake the feeling that she was being followed. For the first mile or so, she constantly checked the trail behind her, but nothing was there. It was probably just her imagination working overtime. Riding alone in the middle of nowhere was not her normal activity. No wonder she'd be apprehensive. In point of fact, it was not a bad idea to continue being extra cautious.

She set a fast pace, having no intention of spending a night on the trail, and arrived in Crimshaw after dark.

The town was less than impressive. A mining town, it consisted of very few buildings cobbled together haphazardly along both sides of the single street. She passed the mine on the way in. In the darkness, the rough sign in front of the shaft opening was its only identifying feature. Having no interest in it or what it produced, Randi passed without stopping. Her objective was the town and, in particular, the law officer there. She hoped he would remember Pearce and be able to point her in his direction.

Only moonlight lit her way down the street until she approached the saloon. That building seemed to have the only activity in Crimshaw. Light emanated from it, but it was not enough to illuminate the street. Sounds of muffled conversations came from inside. Randi rode on, straining her eyes to seek out the law officer's quarters. It was late, but she might as well get this over with now.

A little farther down the street, a white sign with black lettering was visible on the front of a small building. The larger size of the marker caught her eye. She stopped and stared at it, finally deciphering it in the darkness. *City Marshal*, it read. They had a lot of nerve calling this a city. It was not even a village.

Directing her horse to the front of the building, she found no hitch rail. She saw nothing to which she could tie the animal off. She hadn't thought to buy hobbles. She would have to take the chance. She dismounted and slipped the reins over the horse's head, dropping them on the ground. She used a hand signal to illustrate her words. "You stay there." She hoped the horse understood English.

Before moving to the door, Randi brushed trail dust from her clothes and waved her hands in front of her face to keep the stuff out of her eyes and nose. At the door, no light came from inside. Oh, well. She knocked. No response. She knocked again, harder this time.

"I'm coming. I'm coming." The call from inside came from an elderly voice in an annoyed sing-song manner. A second later, a dim light streamed from under the door. Footsteps shuffled inside. The door opened to reveal an older man in a collarless striped shirt and dress trousers. His clean shaven face was long and drawn, lined with age and weather, and his hair was gray, curly, and abundant. He squinted a bit to make out his visitor, and his face registered surprise.

Right, he wasn't expecting a woman or that she'd be wearing trail clothes.

"Well, good evening," he said with a slight smile.

Randi smiled back. "Good evening. Are you the marshal?"

"Why, yes, ma'am. Quentin Lipscomb, that's me."

"How do you do, Marshal? I apologize for the hour, but I've come a long way to see you, and I didn't want to waste any more time."

Lipscomb squinted, apparently scrutinizing her, and then smiled. "Well, young lady, it's not often I get a visit from a pretty lady at any hour. Come on in."

Randi stepped inside. "Thank you."

Lipscomb closed the door and quickly went to the desk in the center of the room to turn up the flame of the coal oil lamp that flickered there. Randi moved farther into the sparsely furnished office.

"I'm Randi Swayze. I'm a Pinkerton agent."

Surprise crossed Lipscomb's face. "You don't say. I didn't know they were hiring women now."

"There are a few of us, yes." She produced her identification.

Lipscomb scratched his head as he viewed it. "Well, don't that beat all. Oh, wait, where're my manners?" He gestured to a chair off to the side. "Please, have a seat."

"Thank you." Randi went to the chair and sat with her hands in her lap. "Marshal, I'm tracking an outlaw named Alonzo Pearce. I'm hoping you can help me. I understand you were involved with him about a year ago."

Lipscomb scrunched his face in thought as he leaned against the desk. "Can't say the name's familiar to me. About a year back, you say?"

"Yes, but you might know him by another name, Shawnee."

That brought a definite flash of recollection to the marshal's face, but it disappeared a second later. "I don't think so. I think you were told wrong."

"I should tell you, I'm not looking to arrest him. Pinkerton has been hired to locate him and make him an offer that could lead to amnesty for him. That's the only reason I'm trying to find him."

Lipscomb cast a sideways look at Randi. "Amnesty, you say. Who's offering amnesty?"

"I'm not at liberty to say. Our client wishes to remain anonymous. That means—"

"I know what *anonymous* means, Miss Swayze. You're not dealing with an idiot here."

She'd gone too far. She needed to rectify this before it blew up on her. "I'm sorry, Marshal. I didn't mean to imply that at all."

"Well, maybe I was a tad hasty. I guess it's not often you find an educated man doing a job like this. It's obvious whoever this client of yours is, he's got the funds to afford your investigation and the power to grant amnesty. I'll leave it at that."

This man was wasted in this one-horse town. She kept going. "You're absolutely right. Can you... will you help me?"

Lipscomb nodded. "I can, and I will. I knew him by both names.

He calls himself Shawnee, but he's on a handbill as Pearce. He showed up here one night with a body he came across on the trail. He could have just left it there, but he did the right thing. Turned out the victim was murdered. Now, Shawnee could have just lit out, but he hung around trying to get to the bottom of who the killer was. Said it wasn't right not to do all he could. I won't go into detail, but Shawnee started poking around and, sure enough, he came up with a suspect. I had no evidence, so I couldn't make the arrest. Shawnee, well, let's just say he had his own ways. He set the killer up. After that, I had enough on him to make the arrest and make it stick. Shawnee was set to leave, to go back on the run, but I felt beholden to him. I convinced him to let me help him like he helped me. I sneaked him across the border into Mexico and got a priest I know down there to help make him disappear. Far as I know, he's still down there."

Randi perked up. "I know he's probably safe in Mexico, but I still need to find him. If his record is cleared, he can come back to the states a free man. I really need to talk to that priest. Can you arrange that?"

Lipscomb shrugged. "The last time I talked to *Padre* Cortez was when I brought Shawnee to the mission. I'm not even sure he's still there."

"I need to find out."

"About all I can do is give you directions to the mission. The rest'd be up to you."

Randi smiled. "I can work with that."

4

"WHEN YOU CROSS THE BORDER, you ride straight southwest, got it?"

Lipscomb spoke to Randi in front of his office early the next morning. Randi listened carefully as she tightened her horse's saddle cinch and checked the equipment and supplies lashed to the packhorse that Lipscomb had provided.

"Watch for signs leading to Arispe. The Mission of Santa Maria is halfway between Arispe and the border. It's big enough so you can't miss it. You'll be looking for *Padre* Guillermo Cortez. If he's still there, tell him I sent you. That doesn't mean he'll talk to you, but it might help."

Randi faced the marshal. "Thank you, Marshal."

"I wish you luck. I'd come with you, but I'm needed here."

Randi smiled. "It's all right. I'm used to traveling alone." She picked up the reins and turned to mount, then she turned back to him. "You know, I have to tell you, I think a man like you is wasted in such an out of the way town as this."

"Well, it's like this, when you get to my age and you want to keep working at what you know, you got to take what's offered. The pay's not that bad and folks here appreciate me."

Randi extended a hand to shake his. "And well they should. Goodbye, Marshal."

"You stay safe, Pinkerton lady."

Randi mounted and headed out of the town, leading the pack-horse. As she rode, there was that gnawing sense again that she was not alone. She again passed it off as an overactive imagination as she turned toward the border crossing a few miles away.

After crossing the border, she rode southwest as instructed and tried to keep as straight a path as possible. This became easier once the sun was high enough in the sky. By keeping the sun at her back over her left shoulder, she maintained the course. Surrounded by mountainous regions and, at times, being forced to ride into and over some of the lower mountains, she found herself being moved off track several times. Reorienting the sun to the desired position corrected her each time.

The farther into Mexico she rode, the hotter it seemed to become. It was not simply the normal increase in temperature as the day progressed. It was obviously a warmer climate than the southern United States. Good thing she had plenty of water and her clothes reflected heat rather than absorbed it, for the most part anyway.

At several intervals when a rest stop was necessary, that uneasiness raised its head again. She surveyed all around her but saw nothing out of the ordinary. In fact, she saw nothing at all except the vast Mexican landscape. She moved on.

Lipscomb had estimated the trip to be a day's ride. She hoped he was right. Without the sun to guide her, it would be easy to get lost out here.

As she exited a narrow mountain pass in late afternoon, the mission loomed in front of her. Although she was tired and hungry from the long day, she moved toward her destination with renewed vigor.

The large, adobe-walled complex had a tall wooden door in the front. Above the door was a weather beaten sign that read, *La Misión de Santa Maria*, in faded black paint. Randi rode up to the door and stopped. The metal ring and plate that served as the knocker was situated at about the height of an average man's shoulder. Without dismounting, she leaned down and rapped the ring against the plate twice. The resulting sound was a loud clang. She expected that would rouse someone. She waited.

In a few seconds, the door opened slightly, revealing an old woman in a black veil and a simple gown-type black dress. Her wrinkled face bore a questioning look. "*Sí?*"

Well, this was awkward. Randi didn't know a word of Spanish. "*Padre* Cortez?" She hoped that worked.

The woman nodded. *"Oh, Sí, ven conmiga."*

Randi guessed that meant follow me.

As the woman pulled the door open wider, Randi directed her horse through the doorway while leading the packhorse behind. Before her was a wooden structure with stained glass windows. The steeple above the door had a cross at its pinnacle, identifying it as the church. She looked around to see several buildings that resembled homes scattered about the property. Strange. She only expected a church. This looked like a small village.

The woman led Randi to a small, free-standing one room adobe building beside the church. She stopped at the door and pointed to it. "*Padre* Cortez," she said.

Randi dismounted and grounded the reins. *"Gracias."* Her pronunciation was her best attempt at Spanish, but it betrayed her American accent.

The woman smiled. *"De nada."* She stepped away to return to the entryway as Randi went to the door and knocked.

From inside, a man's voice called, "*Adalante.*" Randi opened the door and stepped in.

The interior was as sparse as the exterior, small and unpainted, with a cot along one wall and a tiny window in the opposite wall. At a simple wood table, an elderly man sat facing the door. He wore the brown robes of a monk with a carved wooden cross secured loosely around his neck by a leather thong. His face was round and covered with a copious white beard and mustache, while his head was bald save for a strip of white hair around the lower portion. He looked up as Randi entered. The dark eyes had a staring quality that seemed to penetrate his visitor. "*Buen día, Señorita. Coma pueda ayudarte?*"

She wished she'd thought this through. How did she communicate with someone when she didn't speak his language? "*No español,*" she said instinctively, her hands going out, palms up as a symbol of exasperation.

"That is of no consequence, my child. I'm quite fluent in English." His accent was almost non-existent.

Randi smiled. "Lucky for me you are."

The priest smiled back. "How can I help you?" He folded his hands and rested them on the table.

Randi approached. "My name is Randi Swayze. I'm an investigator with the Pinkerton Detective Agency."

Padre Cortez leaned forward. "How very intriguing. An investigator. A *woman* investigator, to boot."

"Yes, sir. I'm seeking a man—an American. Young, good with the gun and the rope, riding a gray horse, I've been told you can help me."

"And who has told you that?"

"Marshal Lipscomb, across the border in Crimshaw."

"Yes, I'm familiar with him. And who is it that you seek?"

"Alonzo Pearce, also known as Shawnee."

The priest's expression turned to one of concern. "I'm afraid I can't help you."

This was going badly. She had to save it. "When I said I'm seeking him, I didn't mean to arrest him. Our client wants to offer him amnesty if he'll come back to the states and help resolve a serious situation. The client has the funds and the power to carry this out, and he's completely trustworthy. This is a chance for Mister Pearce to return to his homeland in freedom."

"I don't suppose you can tell me who your client is."

"No, I can't." Randi hoped that didn't scuttle it.

"All right, let me see if I understand this. You seek this man because your client, a powerful man who must remain unknown, wants to offer him amnesty if he will—"

Randi finished the statement. "Risk his life to do something that no one else has been able to do, yes. I realize I'm asking a lot, but this is very important. The fate of a lot of people depends on whether he agrees to do this or not."

Padre Cortez paused, apparently conflicted. He leaned back in his chair. "Miss Swayze, please have a seat." He gestured to a chair in the corner of the room. "I have to think about this and pray for guidance." He rose and walked to the door. As he let himself out, Randi moved to the chair and sat heavily.

Seconds later, the old woman entered without knocking. She held a clay goblet which she presented to Randi. "*Agua?*"

Recognizing the Spanish word for water, Randi took the cup. "Thank... eh, *gracias.*"

"*De nada.*" The woman turned and left the room as Randi sipped the liquid, quenching the thirst she just realized was there.

She remained in the chair for what seemed to be much longer than the fifteen minutes that actually passed. Her mind wandered back to the journey from Crimshaw and that nagging feeling she was being followed. Who would be following her? For what reason? Could it have something to do with Pearce, or was it just a figment of the overactive imagination of a woman alone in rough country?

As she pondered this, the priest returned, approaching her with an expressionless face.

"I've thought and prayed hard," he said. "And I've decided to tell you what I can about Lon."

Randi got up to face him. "I promise you I don't want to harm him."

Cortez nodded. "I believe you. The marshal brought him here about a year ago. Immediately, he insisted on working for his keep. He did everything he could. After a few months, an intruder came, an American bounty hunter intent on taking Lon back with him across the border. Lon hid from this man, not wanting to bring violence to the mission. To protect Lon, I lied. I convinced the bounty hunter Lon was not here, and the man finally left. Lon told me he had to go where his troubles would involve only himself. He said he was going to the tallest mountain in the area to live alone. It was the only way he could be sure he would not bring harm to others. It would just be Lon and his horse, Gray. As far as I know, he's still there, but I have had no contact with him since he left."

"Can you show me where this mountain is?"

"I can. Come with me."

They stepped outside, and *Padre* Cortez pointed to the southeast. "There it is." His finger drew her eye to a tall summit in the distance, sitting between two shorter peaks.

"How far would you say it is?"

"Half a day's ride on a good horse should get you there. I can't say how long it will take to get to the top or exactly where he might be. Some people who live in the area say they've seen smoke coming from close to the peak. That might be Lon."

Randi looked around at the sun waning in the west. Foolish to start now. Morning would be cooler, and she wouldn't lose daylight. "*Padre*, would it be all right if I stay here overnight and get a fresh start in the morning?"

Cortez smiled. "Exactly what I was about to suggest. I'll have a room readied for you. Will you do me the honor of taking supper with me?"

Randi smiled back. "Thank you. I'd like that."

"Come," he said as he gestured to another building to the side of the church.

She walked with him. "*Padre*, I'm curious. May I ask you how you came to know English so well?"

He chuckled. "Oh, that's simple. I was born and raised in New York."

―――――――――

EARLY THE NEXT MORNING, RANDI prepared to head out on the trip to what she hoped would be Pearce's location. She took from her packhorse's rigging only a supply of beef jerky and two canteens filled with fresh water from the mission's well. Leaving the pack-horse at the mission would help to speed up her journey. *Padre* Cortez agreed to stable the horse until she returned. She mounted, thanked Cortez for his hospitality, and set out.

As she left the mission, she again experienced that underlying feeling that she was not alone. A glance around her provided no information, but it also did not allay the suspicion. Still, she set the pace at slightly less than a canter to keep from wearing out the horse. She zeroed in on the mountain and tried to keep as straight a line as possible, keeping that high peak in constant sight. The trail, nothing more than a route that had been beaten down over time into the semblance of a road, wound left and right to circumvent outcroppings of rock. She navigated these turns and managed each time to again locate and continue toward the mountain.

After an hour of sustained riding, she reached an open plain area. Again that foreboding. It was more prevalent now. She looked around again. There was something back there, or someone. She saw nothing, but she knew it was there. Looking ahead, she approached another maze of rock formations. Time to resolve this, whatever it was.

She increased speed slightly, not enough to raise alarm, but enough to reach the rocks well ahead of her supposed pursuer. Around the first bend, she glanced back to be sure she could not be seen, then went to a gallop to reach a scalable formation. Without hesitation, she directed her horse up a narrow, stone strewn path that led to a depression in the rock large enough to fit horse and rider. Its length seemed about a hundred feet, its trajectory erratic, its steep angle threatening. The horse stumbled a time or two, almost spilling her once, but it made the climb, putting Randi behind a shielding boulder that hid both from the trail below. She crouched low enough to be concealed. Peering around the side of the boulder allowed her a view of the trail. Lifting the revolver from its holster, she waited.

Quickened breath, increased heartbeat. Mouth dry too. She'd never been involved in an actual gunfight. Nearby, yes. Almost involved, yes. But this close to the inevitable, no. And not alone. Remember the training. Don't expose yourself. Maintain the advantage. Make sure you're in range. Make your shots count. That's what Dad taught. His being a police officer didn't hurt. The times out in back of the house with him, learning to shoot, they helped as well. Stay calm. Stay in command.

Randi's field of vision went back to the last turn she had taken to arrive at her current point. Coming around that bend, a lone rider hurried along the trail. He was stocky and wore a dark floppy hat and a light colored duster that reached to his boot tops. She could not make out his features. He approached the path she had used to ascend the boulders. She pulled in a breath and shouted, "That's far enough. Stop where you are."

The man pulled up sharply.

Randi settled her gun's front sight upon him. "Would you mind telling me just *why* you're following me, sir?"

He sat mute in the saddle.

"I'm warning you." She tried to control the nervousness in her voice. "I've got a gun aimed right at you. Why are you following me?"

Seeming to pay her no heed, he looked around without replying. Then, suddenly, he urged his horse forward, dismounted on the run and made for the cover of boulders on the side of the trail. Randi followed him with the barrel of her Colt.

Dropping behind a boulder, the man came up with a handgun and fired one shot in Randi's general direction. The shot hit nothing. She flinched at the sound, but did not return fire. Probably trying to flush me out. Don't give away your position.

"Hey, up there," the man shouted. "You take me to Pearce and I'll split the reward with you. Half's better'n none at all. What do you say?"

So that was it. He was a bounty hunter. How did he find out about this? She must've been right about him being back there all along. He probably tailed her all the way from Crimshaw. Maybe earlier. How did he stay hidden so well and still stay with her? "I'm not interested," she said. "I don't want the reward."

"You're shitting me, lady. Why else would you be here?" As he called out, he moved slightly to find a better shooting position.

Randi watched him carefully, still holding aim on him. "That's none of your business. Now get out of here before I start shooting."

The man laughed. "You ain't got the piss and vinegar for that. I can hear it in your voice." He located a channel and began climbing toward her.

"Back off." She tried to steady her voice. "Get out of here."

Again he laughed as he pegged another shot, this time bouncing the bullet off the rock face close to Randi's cover.

He was zeroing in, and he was not stopping. Got to do it. She renewed her aim as he climbed. She staged the double action trigger halfway back and squeezed. The gun spat a .38 slug that took a chunk out of the man's upper arm, his gun arm. He lost his revolver, missed a stone under his foot and rolled and tumbled down the path to level ground.

Randi stood up and started to descend toward him. Before she could get very far, he scrambled to his feet, his left hand gripping his right arm below the wound, and trotted to his horse across the trail. He gathered the reins and hauled himself into the saddle. With a quick yank, he pulled the horse around and went to a gallop heading back the way he came.

Randi stopped. Must have hit him. There was blood on his coat. She aimed another shot at him, but missed because of the movement of his horse. That should at least keep him running. She pushed a long breath of relief through her lips, pursing them out in a pucker, as the man rounded the bend at full gallop and was gone.

For a long moment, she stood in the same spot, regaining her composure, waiting for the adrenaline rush to pass. She'd held her own in a gunfight! She'd survived. Maybe she'd even come out on top. Not bad for a Pinkerton lady from Minneapolis.

Remembering one of her father's lessons, she opened the loading gate on the Colt Lightning and ejected the two spent shells. She turned to climb back up to where her horse was waiting and reached into the saddlebag for ammunition. She crouched and opened the box with her right hand while holding the gun in her left. Quickly, she replaced live rounds into the empty chambers and holstered the weapon. After putting the box away, she mounted and eased the horse down the rough path to the trail. Without stopping, she increased speed to continue toward the mountain and her objective of finding Pearce.

5

SNAPPING OUT OF HER REVERIE about three quarters of the way up the mountain, a cabin came into Randi's view. It was ramshackle, built of logs, with a rudimentary adobe roof. No windows were visible. The road seemed to end at the cabin. A big gray horse, unsaddled, was picketed nearby, indicating Pearce might live there. *Padre* Cortez indicated Pearce rode a horse he called Gray. Could be.

As a precaution, she pulled rein and drew her sidearm to check the loads, just to make sure, just in case. It wasn't that long since she had used the weapon, but Randi had learned one can't be too careful or too thorough. She kept the weapon low and close to her body to prevent the nickel plated finish from reflecting the sun and signaling her presence. Satisfied, she holstered the gun and resumed riding, coming to within a quarter mile of the cabin.

At that point, she reined in and dismounted, leading her horse off the road to tie the reins on a stout branch. She moved toward the cabin, staying close to the wooded area along the road. This helped to keep her hidden. Her movement was careful, avoiding loose stones and branches.

The rude little cabin was in the middle of a clearing with woods all around it, but she would have to cross several feet of open area to reach the building.

Well, she'd come this far. She had to see this through.

Placing her hand on the butt of the revolver to prevent it from jostling out, she went to a run across the clearing and came to a stop at the makeshift door. She contemplated her next action.

Should she knock or just barge in?

"Can I help you, ma'am?"

The voice behind her startled her enough to make her visibly jump and pull in a sharp breath. She recovered quickly. Male, deep, American. Possibly... probably Pearce. Her glance to the left showed her a stocky man of medium height wearing the clothes of an American cowboy, right down to the chaps. She wondered how he tolerated that in this heat? He resembled the image she had seen on the wanted posters.

Well, here went nothing! "Mister Pearce?"

Uncharacteristically, her voice cracked.

"They call me Shawnee, ma'am." There was a smirk on his face.

"Yes, I know, but you *are* Alonzo Pearce, aren't you?" Might as well get that out of the way up front.

"Shawnee, ma'am, just Shawnee is all."

Randi turned to face him fully. There was no sense putting him on the defensive this early in the game. "All right, Shawnee then. I was very careful. How did you know I was here?"

"See that gray over there? He's nigh-on to fifteen years, but his ears still work real good. He heard you coming, maybe half a mile down the trail. Lets me know when he hears things. He's good like that."

Randi got the impression that he felt a bit awkward. She didn't expect that. "I see. I didn't account for a talking horse." Flippant, maybe, but maybe it would lighten the exchange.

Shawnee's smile broadened. "He's got his own way of talking. But I surely didn't account for a lady bounty hunter. Reckon now I seen just about everything." His left hand went behind his neck in a gesture of wonder, but his right hand never strayed very far from the gun situated on his hip.

"I'm not a bounty hunter, Shawnee. Why do you think I am?"

"Matter of ciphering is all. Being a lady aside, you ain't likely the law. This here's Mexico. American law don't apply here. The law'd know that and not bother sending nobody down here. About the only thing left is the price on my head. Must be close to a thousand by now. That kind of cash draws bounty hunters. You ain't the first, but, being a lady, you surely be the differentist."

Shawnee was talking more than Randi expected. He probably got very little company up here if any. Good. Keep him talking.

"I'm not a bounty hunter, Shawnee. My name is Randi Swayze. I'm a Pinkerton agent. I'm not here to arrest you. I've come with an offer for you that very well could change your life." As she spoke, she put her hands out, palms down, to indicate a non-threatening move, then slowly reached into her skirt pocket for her identification wallet. She displayed it plainly enough and long enough for him to read.

Shawnee studied the document. "Reckon you be a honest-to-God Pinkerton man—lady, all right. Case you ain't noticed, though, my life was already changed back a ways, and it weren't for the better. What makes you think I'd want it changed again?"

Randi pocketed the wallet. "Because, this time, it could change for the better."

Shawnee appeared to be scrutinizing her, looking her up and down, so much so that she became uncomfortable and fidgeted. After a few seconds of this, she broke the silence. "Why are you staring at me? Is something wrong?"

"You surely are tall... for a lady, that is."

"Oh." Her voice went up another octave, betraying her amazement at his notice.

He seemed to pick up on that. "I didn't mean nothing by it. Sorry if I made you uneasy. Been a while since I seen a woman, and you being tall and ladylike and all... just a compliment is all. Shoot—just forget I said anything."

His stumbling manner immediately put her at ease. "No, it's all right. Thank you."

He smiled awkwardly. "Yes, ma'am. Look, would you want to get on out of this sun, come inside and set a spell? It's cooler inside."

His boyish quality charmed her. "Yes, I'd like that."

He stepped closer and reached past her to lift the door latch. A gentle shove swung the door open on squawking hinges. He made a gesture with his hand, a silent invitation to enter.

She walked into a darkened room, the lighting of which seemed to be provided only by the spaces between the horizontal logs that made up the walls. The irregular shapes of the logs did not quite line up, allowing light to leak through. In front of her, in the middle of the single room, a rudimentary wood table and two equally makeshift wood chairs were placed on one side. A ragged pinstriped mattress lay in the far corner, the darkest part of the room. A single coal oil lamp was somehow attached to the far wall at eye level. The rest of the room was bare.

Randi immediately immersed herself in the rustic simplicity of the cabin, allowing herself to imagine the hardships he endured. She was brought back to reality when Shawnee entered behind her and walked to a side wall. He lifted a latch situated at shoulder level and released a swing-out panel that was apparently the only semblance of a window in the structure. Daylight streamed in, brightening the room to a dim light that was enough to see and move around.

"If we leave the door open," he said. "it'll cool the place down some." He pulled out one of the chairs. "Here. Sit down."

She sat tentatively. He took the seat across from her.

"Is this your... home?"

"Yes, ma'am. Well, sort of. It ain't much, but it's shelter."

She turned in the chair and leaned onto the table. It was time to get into this deeper. "Shawnee, some of the things you've done, the good things I've learned about, show you to be more than just a wanted outlaw."

"Well, I've surely tried. Didn't think nobody noticed."

"They've noticed. But, for all that good, don't you want more than... this?" She gestured to indicate his meager existence as she shrugged.

"I reckon, but that ain't possible."

"Actually, it might be. You're an American citizen. For all the hardships you've had up north, do you really want to spend the rest of your life in a foreign country, alone on the top of a mountain?"

"Lesser of two evils." He leaned back in the chair. It creaked under his weight. "Stay here and just deal with bounty hunters from time to time, or go back across the border and deal with every lawman west of the Mississippi and bounty hunters as well. Easy choice."

"What if you could become a free man, absolved of all the crimes you're accused of? Wouldn't you want that?"

"What're you getting at here? Ain't nobody going to just wipe out the past like that."

"The governor of New Mexico Territory has the power to do just that."

Shawnee showed interest, leaning forward toward the table. The chair creaked again. "How's that?"

"Governor Wallace is faced with a serious outlaw problem in the territory. He's tried everything legal to stop them. Everything has failed. He's beside himself and is now willing to go outside the law to stop them. He's looking for a wanted outlaw to seek them out and join them. If this person can bring them down, he's offering amnesty, a clean slate. The person he has in mind is you. That's why I've spent four months tracking you down, to make you that offer."

Shawnee looked astounded. "Hah! Why me?"

"Of that I'm not sure, but when he gave us the assignment, he specifically asked for you... by name."

"Which name?"

"Both."

"Reckon he knows somebody that knows me, 'cause I surely don't know him."

"You did come recommended. He said as much."

"Hah!" He was quiet, contemplative for a few seconds.

Randi decided to push this further. "Shawnee, will you consider the offer?"

He remained quiet another few seconds, then he leaned back in the creaking chair and pushed his hat to the back of his head. "Yes, ma'am. Reckon I'll ponder on it."

For a few seconds which seemed like much longer to Randi, Shawnee stared in her direction. She couldn't tell if he was staring at her or just off into space. She guessed that was how he "pondered."

Randi broke the silence. "Would it be all right if I fetched my horse and tied him off with yours? He could probably use some water."

"Sure thing."

She got up and turned toward the doorway.

"You surely are mannerly and all, ma'am, asking permission like you done," he said offhandedly. "Never expected a Pinkerton to act like that."

"Thank you," she said sincerely.

"Yes, ma'am."

Randi stepped outside, a grin on her face, impressed by Shawnee's chivalry.

GRAY WHINNIED AND NODDED ITS head as Randi approached. She had brought her horse alongside Gray to tie off its reins and provide it with water, and now she ventured closer to Gray. Taken with the horse's size and beauty, she attempted to get acquainted. Gray permitted the closeness.

"You're a good-looking one, aren't you?" Randi said softly as her hands caressed Gray's head and neck.

"He usually don't allow that of strangers," Shawnee said from behind Randi. "Reckon he approves of you."

"Well, I certainly approve of him."

"Yeah, he's a good friend." Shawnee joined her. "Look, ma'am, I done thought about what you said. How do I know you ain't some slick article looking to lure me across the border into a trap, maybe a posse just waiting to get their hands on me?"

Randi looked him squarely in the eye. "Because I swear to you that's not true."

"And I'm supposed to just believe you?"

"Shawnee, I'm not lying to you. I've made the offer exactly as Governor Wallace stated it to Mister Pinkerton. If you can stop these raids, the governor will make you a free man again."

"If I live through it."

"Yes, there is that." Randi moved her hand to Gray's nose and stroked it. "And that's the decision only you can make. Is it worth risking your life for a chance to have your life back?"

"What do you get if I say yes?"

"My job was to find you and make the offer. I've done that. Whether I take you to the governor or go back empty-handed, I still get paid. I'm not going to try to sway you one way or the other. I just want you to believe the offer is genuine."

Shawnee nodded. "This governor, Wallace, is he the general, Lew Wallace, the Union Army general?"

Randi nodded. "The very same."

"Yeah, I heard of him. Good man." Shawnee looked off into the woods and stood there for a long moment while Randi continued to stroke Gray. "You hungry?" he asked without looking at her.

She looked at him and cocked her head. "I guess," she said tentatively. She hadn't really thought about food.

He turned, smiling. "Well, good. I got a deer carcass in the shed out back. Took it down this morning. We ought to eat good if we're going to be riding a spell." With that, he walked back toward the cabin.

"Where are we riding to?"

"Well, shoot," he called over his shoulder. "Ain't we got to go on up New Mexico way?"

6

A WOODEN SHED SAT AT the tree line behind the cabin. Midway between the cabin and the shed, a fire pit was built in the clearing. A makeshift roasting spit, over the pit, bore a butchered deer carcass. The remnants of the extinguished fire still emitted smoke as Randi and Shawnee sat nearby finishing the meals. It was close to midafternoon.

"Reckon we'll start out fresh in the morning," Shawnee said. "You can take the mattress tonight. I'll sleep outside."

"All right." Randi was immediately reassured by his words that she would be safe with him. He had been open and honest with her up to now. No reason to think that would change.

"I'll cut up some of this meat and salt it down to preserve it," he said. "Come in handy on the trip."

"I can help with that. By the way, I left a packhorse and provisions at the mission. We can stop there and get them."

Shawnee grinned and nodded. "Good thinking. We can carry more with us that-a-way. Takes the load off the riding horses." He pulled the knife from its seat in the roasted meat and began slicing.

They salted the cuts thoroughly and wrapped them in strips he cut from the deer skin that lay drying in the clearing. He found leather thongs in his saddlebag and tied the packages. The balance of the skin provided a sack to contain the parcels. He tied this off at the top.

"We'll eat pretty good for a spell," he said.

She looked at him and chuckled at the thought behind her next statement. "You really thought I was a bounty hunter?"

"Up to now, weren't many other possibles. In a way, though, you are a hunter, just not the bounty kind."

"I guess you're right. By the way, since we're talking about bounty hunters, on the way up here, I had a run-in with a man who I think is one. He trailed me all the way from Crimshaw. I confronted him a short distance from here. We traded shots, and I wounded him enough to chase him away."

"You didn't kill him?"

"No." She was repelled by the question.

"Then he ain't gone."

"But he was wounded. I saw the blood on his arm when he ran."

"Don't matter. He's in it for the money. Long as he can still walk, he ain't backing off. I dealt with enough of that kind in my time to know how they think. They're like wolves. Don't let go. Likely be laying for us on the trail somewheres."

"I wounded him, and he ran. I couldn't just shoot him down."

"Don't know if you could or not. What I'm telling you is, somebody shoots at you, you shoot back. You shoot to kill, 'cause if you don't, he'll surely kill you, or try to, sooner or later."

Picking up the sack of meat, Shawnee walked away from the fire pit, toward the house.

"Shawnee, I'm not a killer," Randi called after him.

"Most nobody is… till they are."

Darkness rolled in as they finished setting up for their trip. Finding herself exhausted from the rigors of this day, Randi decided to turn in early. To facilitate this, Shawnee gathered his bedding from the cabin and set it down outside. Randi occupied the mattress without concern for her safety. He arranged his bedroll halfway between the cabin and the picket line. Both slept soundly through the night.

At first light, Randi awoke with a start. She looked around at the strange surroundings before returning to full awareness of her situation. Throwing back the blanket, she got to her feet and stretched the remnants of sleep from her body. She yawned as she reached for her boots. After pulling them on, she ventured outside to a slightly chilly dawn. Immediately, a combination of campfire and coffee reached her nostrils. She sniffed a time or two and then followed the smell to its source.

As she rounded the corner of the cabin, Shawnee sat with his back to her at the fire pit. A small restarted fire burned inside a ring of stones that bore a steaming coffee pot.

"Morning," he said without turning. "You're just in time. Coffee's ready."

"How did you know I was back here?" she asked as she approached.

"Gray ain't the only one hears things."

Randi crouched and took the tin cup he handed her. "I guess you have to, to stay alive."

"Mighty well told."

They drank coffee and ate venison for breakfast. The meal progressed in silence until, at its conclusion, Shawnee spoke up.

"They's a stream just on through the woods there," he said, pointing past the shed. "You can wash up, you're a mind. Water's cold, but it's clear enough."

"Sounds good." Randi rose and moved carefully through the woods. The gurgling of the stream reached her before she got to it. As she stepped out of the wood line, the runoff from higher up on the mountain presented an inviting picture and full sound of crystal clear rushing water.

She went to the bank and knelt down, dipping cupped hands into the flowing liquid. The coldness on her skin sent a chill up her spine, but she accepted the challenge and splashed the stuff onto her face. For a second, it took her breath away, but she welcomed the bracing result as water dribbled onto her blouse. A contented smile crossed her face. She wasn't sure if the water or the success of the search drove that, but both were good things.

"Hey, ma'am," Shawnee called from inside the wood line. "I come to fill the canteens. I can wait if you ain't decent."

How gallant of him to check first. He never ceased to surprise. "No, it's fine. Come ahead."

Shawnee moved through the woods and emerged, carrying several canteens, including the two from Randi's saddle. He set them down, uncapped them and began filling them in the stream. As he finished each, Randi took it from him and replaced the stopper.

"You know," she said offhandedly. "If we're going to be riding together for a few weeks, can you please stop calling me ma'am? My name is Randi."

Shawnee did not look up. "Sure thing... Randi. Nice name. Fits you."

She smiled. "Thanks."

"Long as we're talking names, you go ahead on and call me Lon. Been a month of Sundays since I been called that."

"I'd be happy to... Lon."

————————

THEY PACKED UP AND RODE out with Shawnee in the lead. On the narrow trail down the mountain, Randi stayed about a horse's length behind. Shawnee set a slow, steady pace and kept a sharp eye out for anything out of the ordinary, whether animal or human. To the best of her ability, Randi did the same, but she trusted Shawnee's superior instincts and skills over her own.

They reached level ground without incident. Now, on a wider trail, Randi came along Shawnee's side. They rode silently into the mountainous area near Randi's encounter with the bounty hunter.

"Up ahead, that's where I stopped the bounty hunter," Randi said.

Shawnee slowed the pace to a walk, scouring the rocks for any sign of danger, movement, or perhaps the presence of a weapon. They rounded the turn where Randi hid from the tracker. As they came out of the bend, Gray shook its head and let out a low whinny. Shawnee pulled up immediately. Randi followed suit.

"There's something up ahead. Some*one*, actually." Shawnee nodded, patting Gray's neck.

Randi strained her eyes. "I don't see anything."

"He's hid, laying for us. Gray knows he's there."

Another curve loomed ahead of them. Shawnee dismounted and handed Gray's reins over to her. He then pulled the rifle from its saddle scabbard.

"You stay here. *Right* here," he pointed to the spot on the ground. "I'm going up top. When I signal you, send Gray on ahead, going fast."

"I don't understand."

"Gray'll draw him out, keep his attention for a bit. Makes the hunter the hunted."

Randi nodded, realizing he had this figured out already. Her eyes followed Shawnee as he climbed the rock face, expertly placing his feet in secure spots. He moved carefully along the top, crouching to present the smallest target. She guessed the distance at an eighth of a mile up.

He reached a point just past the curve and stopped. After scanning ahead, he waved the rifle above his head. Randi took that to be the signal. She slapped Gray's hindquarters hard with an open hand. The horse went to an immediate gallop around the bend and disappeared from her view. She waited.

Tense minutes passed. As a precaution, Randi drew her sidearm. A man's voice called out in the distance, possibly Shawnee's. She heard two shots, in rapid succession, sounded. The first was a shorter, lower-pitched resonance, a revolver. The second, a higher, sharper crack, a rifle. She hoped that was Shawnee's rifle. Everything went silent.

More time passed. She could not tell the duration. She waited impatiently. Then a third shot came the revolver again. And nothing from the rifle, indicating he might be in trouble.

Randi raised the Colt to shoulder height and extended her arm, ready to fire. Her breath quickened. A second passed. The rifle fired in the distance again, and all the sounds stopped. No creature. No wind.

Agonizing minutes later, with Randi still in her fire-ready position, the sound of a horse's hooves approaching started faintly and became louder. Gray, with Shawnee mounted, came around the curve. Randi lifted the gun skyward and holstered it as Shawnee stopped in front of her. His face was expressionless, telling her nothing.

"Are you... well, all right?" She did not attempt to hide the concern in her voice.

"Yup."

"What happened up there?"

Shawnee smiled. "He missed. I didn't."

THEY CONTINUED THE JOURNEY, RIDING side by side, without pausing to locate and examine the bounty hunter's body. Both were silent.

Randi's curiosity about the details of the encounter ran wild, but she read in Shawnee's demeanor that he preferred not to discuss it. She left it alone until, several miles on, she could no longer contain it. But she tried a different approach, not a direct question.

"I could have helped back there, you know."

He spoke while looking straight ahead. "Maybe, maybe not. Said it yourself, you ain't a killer. Thing like that back there, you got to be. Can't second guess. Just got to do it. Look, I want you safe. We run into anything else, you stay behind me. I'll handle it. Savvy?"

Randi read more into those words than Shawnee said. There was concern there for her. He wanted her safe. Maybe he cared for her. That was better left alone for now. "Yes... I do."

They were silent again until they reached the mission later in the day. With the complex in sight, Shawnee called a halt. Randi pulled up beside him.

"You get the packhorse," he said. "I'll go on up ahead and wait on you."

"I thought you'd want to see the *padre* again. Isn't he a friend?"

"He is. Last time I was here, it didn't go good. No point in a second visit. 'Sides, out here, I can see if somebody trails you when you leave."

"I'm certain only one was following me."

"Out here, ain't nothing certain. You go on."

Randi accepted his wisdom and directed her horse toward the mission. As she approached the big door, it swung open—as if she was expected. She rode through the opening. The old woman stood beside the door, ready to close it. Ahead, *Padre* Cortez stood outside the door to his quarters. Randi drew her rein and dismounted nearby.

"Good day, Miss Swayze," the priest said with a smile. "We saw you coming."

Randi held on to her reins and moved closer to him. "Good day to you, *Padre*. I wondered about that."

"I'm glad to see you're safe. Did you find Lon?"

"Yes, I did. He's going back with me."

"That's good. I pray it works out for him. And he didn't want to stop here?"

"No. I think he's concerned for your safety if you're with him."

Cortez was pensive. "Yes, I can see that. Lon is quite a conflicted young man, but he has his principles, and he stands by them."

"I've noticed that. It impresses me. If you don't mind, I'd like to get my packhorse. Lon is waiting for me on the trail."

"Of course. I'll help you."

They walked to the stable where the packhorse was lodged. The priest helped Randi load the pack saddle and rigging to the animal and secure it in place. They repacked her supplies onto the horse and secured them.

Cortez followed as Randi led both horses out of the stable area. She extended her hand and he shook it.

"It's been a pleasure knowing you, Miss Swayze. You're doing a good thing here. I bless you for it." He made the sign of the cross in front of her.

Touched by the gesture, Randi smiled. "Thank you, *Padre*. That's high praise coming from you."

"*Vaya con Dios, niña.*"

7

USK SETTLED IN AS RANDI and Shawnee approached the border crossing, which was marked by a stone pillar about three feet high embedded in the ground. Chiseled into the stone, on the Mexican side, the single word, *México*. On the opposite side, *USA*.

Shawnee called a halt and pointed to a small building a half mile before the crossing site. "Border up ahead. You go on through. I'll find another way to meet you on the other side."

"How will I find you in the dark?"

"Keep heading north. I'll find you."

Shawnee clucked at Gray and pulled the reins to the right. He entered some bushes on the trail's side and was gone. Randi rode on toward the hut.

About two hundred yards south of the pillar, a tiny wood hut, painted white, stood on the side of the road. A similar enclosure stood approximately the same distance north of the stone.

Outside the structure on the Mexican side, two men in the khaki uniforms of the Mexican Army sat leisurely in wood chairs.

The process of crossing the border, from the time she reached the Mexican hut to the point at which she exited the U.S. facility, consumed about twenty minutes during which darkness displaced dusk. Randi spent most of that period bridging the language barrier with the Mexican soldiers. She left the American installation and rode north on a well-traveled trail for about a mile, constantly looking around for any sign of Shawnee. As she started up a slight rise, a few yards ahead, a shadowed figure on horseback entered the trail from the bushes. He stopped in the center of the trail and waited. While she could not make out the man's features, the outline of rider and horse framed in the moonlight gave enough indication it was Shawnee that she continued toward him.

"I found a good campsite."

He led the way into the bushes and up a gentle hill to a flat area that was bounded on three sides by a fifty foot rock wall. Affording a full view of the trail to their front, the spot offered the protection of the wall behind them. They fed and cared for the horses and settled in for the night, maintaining a cold camp. The sight of a fire this close to the border might invite unwanted company.

Early the next morning, their breakfast was deer jerky, the same food that served as the previous night's meal.

"Going to be getting rough from here on," Shawnee said as they saddled up. "Nothing but high country 'tween here and Santa Fe."

"Then I'll need to stop somewhere to send a telegram to the governor telling him we're on our way."

"Fort Craig's the only place I know of near here has a telegraph. You can stop there."

They mounted and set out, going north and keeping to the underbrush and away from well-traveled roads. Within a day, they approached Fort Craig. Shawnee drew rein about a half mile away. Randi stopped beside him.

"Far as I go," Shawnee said. "I'll wait here for you. Careful what you tell the governor."

"It'll be only one word, emissary. It's a code he arranged with Mister Pinkerton. It tells him we're coming without telling him we're coming, just in case someone else sees the message."

Shawnee nodded. "Good thinking."

"Yeah, we're pretty thorough," Randi said as she rode on alone.

A short time later, after sending the cryptic message, Randi rejoined Shawnee. They skirted around the fort, staying far enough away to keep out of the view of the sentries, and then turned northeast to the foothills of the Black Mountains which paralleled the Upper Rio Grande River.

"We'll keep the river in sight as we go and watch for an easier crossing point," Shawnee said as they approached the mountains. "One way or t'other, we going to get wet 'fore we get to Santa Fe."

Randi flashed a forced smile, but made no comment. The prospect of fording the river held no attraction. She followed Shawnee into the hills.

The incline began slowly, then quickly became a thirty degree climb over uneven, difficult to navigate, rocky passages. Care had to be taken in directing the horses to avoid missteps. This slowed their progress to a walk.

Randi's horse began showing signs of skittishness, making the animal more of a handful to control. Shawnee held back from the lead position and rode alongside Randi. Randi noticed a calmer demeanor in her horse. She wasn't sure if Lon or Gray caused it, but she welcomed it all the same.

After an hour of this tedium, Shawnee called a halt to rest the horses. The sound of rushing water reached them.

"There's the Rio Grande down there." He pointed to their right at the great crashing waterway below them.

Sheer cliffs created canyon walls leading down to the river. Randi tried to gauge the distance between their position and the water's surface but could not. In truth, she preferred to leave that question unanswered.

"We've got to cross that?" Her voice showed disbelief.

"We ain't there just yet. It gets narrower up north. Calms down a mite, as well."

"I still can't say I'm looking forward to it."

"Yeah, same here, but we'll be all right. Don't worry, I done it before. I'll keep you safe."

Continuing their journey, with stops for rest, they followed the steep grade leading to the top of the mountain range. Once there, the terrain leveled off. Shawnee located a path through the rocks that allowed easier passage. At this altitude, the air became lighter, making it more difficult for riders and horses to breathe. It sapped their strength more rapidly.

Determined to see this through, Randi stayed at Shawnee's side and tried to duplicate his actions. Her horse continued its fearful reactions, but the close presence of Shawnee and Gray kept the animal manageable.

The path led to a point at which a rock wall to their left rose at least twenty feet above them. To the right, a ledge began a drop straight down to the river below. The way forward was an uneven rock shelf about six feet wide that led to an open area about ten feet away.

Shawnee's scan of the area to find a safer way across quickly proved futile. "Looks like the only way."

"Let's do it," Randi said uncertainly, trying to bolster her confidence with words that did not help.

Shawnee moved Gray up into the lead position to cross the ridgeline. "Stay close, now."

Randi nudged her heels on her horse's flanks. The animal moved forward, falling in behind Gray, as Randi tugged on the packhorse's reins. Slowly, the party moved ahead.

Entering the confines of the ledge, Randi's horse shied, attempting to back up, then trying to turn around. Randi pulled on the reins to straighten the horse's direction, but fear gripped the animal. With frightened whinnies, it reared and stomped, leaning toward the wall to get away from the edge.

Reacting to the noise, Shawnee glanced behind him. As Randi's horse hugged the wall, scraping her leg against the sharp rock face, Shawnee stopped Gray and dismounted. Randi struggled to regain control of the horse as Shawnee approached slowly, speaking in a calming voice to the animal. "Whoa, there, easy now." He reached out and gripped the halter, using his hand to direct the horse back and away from the wall, keeping himself between the horse and the edge. Then, continuing to use his calming voice, he moved the horse back slowly.

She watched in fascination as Shawnee walked the horse backward off the ledge, displacing the packhorse at the same time. He held the halter tightly until the horse calmed down a little.

"Get down," he said

She dismounted carefully and handed the reins over. "What was that all about?"

"Reckon he don't like heights, or much of anything else. Where'd you get this fellow?"

"From a stable at Fort Craig on my way south."

"Reckon they didn't do you no favors. We'll have to get him across."

"I don't think he's going to stand for that."

"He will if he don't know what's there."

Randi voiced the question in her mind. "What do you mean?"

"Trick I learned a while back," Shawnee pulled the bandana from around his neck. He looked over his shoulder at the ledge. Gray still stood in the same spot. "Gray. Back, son, back."

Randi watched in awe as Gray slowly moved backward along the ledge until wider ground was reached. Then the horse turned and walked to Shawnee. Gray's presence settled Randi's horse a bit more.

Shawnee spoke comforting words to Randi's horse as he wrapped his bandana across the animal's face over its eyes and tied the ends off on the halter straps.

"Get up on Gray," Shawnee told Randi.

She complied. Shawnee tied her horse's reins to Gray's tail and then mounted the frightened horse.

"Take him across."

Randi started Gray along the ledge, noticing that Gray never faltered. This motion took up the rein slack, pulling Randi's horse forward close to Gray's hindquarters. Slowly, the party moved across to the other side with Shawnee leading the packhorse behind.

Randi did not look back, but could tell from the sounds behind her that her horse gave no trouble throughout the short ride. She breathed a sigh of relief upon reaching the safety of the other side. She and Shawnee dismounted at the same time.

"That was amazing."

"Naw! I just took away what he was scared of. He can't see it, it ain't there. Didn't hurt he was close to Gray as well."

"You're full of tricks, aren't you?"

"Yup, reckon I got to be."

Toward dusk later that day, Shawnee looked for a suitable campsite, selecting a setback in the rock face the overhang of which provided shelter. "We'll camp here tonight and get an early start in the morning."

They went to work immediately to set up camp and, less than a half hour later, a small fire flourished in the center of the clearing. They stripped the horses down, then fed and watered them. The deer meat on the pack saddle provided the evening meal and, as the chill of the night rolled over them, they relaxed by the fire.

With the action open on his Winchester Yellow Boy, Shawnee forced a piece of cloth through the barrel, using a straight branch with the bark scraped away as a cleaning rod.

Randi stretched and yawned. "I'm going to turn in. This has been a long day."

"Set your bedroll up here by the fire. I'll sleep in the bushes back there." He indicated the brush that lined the rock face.

"That's not necessary, Lon. I trust you."

"Ain't a matter of trust." He looked straight at her. "It's right to do."

Randi hesitated. He certainly did have his principles, like the *padre* had told her. "All right."

He closed the action and reloaded the rifle, then got up and moved his gear into the bushes. The sounds of Shawnee's movements as he arranged his bedding reached Randi's ears.

Then there was silence.

Her thoughts drifted back to those elements of his character she had already experienced and coupled them with this occurrence. There was so much more to this man. Talk about a waste, what a waste his years of running made of his life.

"Good night, Lon."

A few seconds later, she heard, "Night, Randi."

————————

THROUGH THE BALANCE OF THE trip the path became less treacherous. There were no more ledges to cross and, while hoof placement on the uneven rocks was still a problem for the horses, the terrain was flatter. As days passed, the river below narrowed as Shawnee predicted, and its current slowed to a steady flow that appeared less dangerous to cross.

After the tenth day, the mountains began a gentle downward grade that brought them closer to the level of the river. At the same time, the waterway narrowed to the point at which, four days later, the eastern bank, their interim destination, could be seen. They turned toward the western bank as the sun was setting behind them. Shawnee called a halt about a hundred feet from the water's edge.

"We'll cross here," he said over the sound of the flowing water. "Santa Fe's a couple miles south."

They moved on to the river bank. Shawnee pulled up and dismounted. "Dog down on that cinch so's the saddle don't slip in the water." He flipped up the left side stirrup and retightened Gray's saddle cinch. Randi got down and did the same. Then he removed his hat and lashed it by its chin chord to the side of Gray's saddle. Randi did not mimic that move, leaving her hat on.

They remounted and slowly started into the water with Shawnee leading the packhorse. Moving at an angle to compensate for the course of the river, they began crossing as the flow attempted to carry them downstream. The soaking of her skirt pulled on Randi's lower body as her horse made its way toward the far bank. The weight of the saturated cloth tended to hold her in her seat, but she still hung on tightly to the saddle horn for additional support.

As they entered the center of the river, the intensity of the current increased. While Gray did not falter, Randi's horse floundered, seemingly overcome by the flow of the water. The animal panicked,

attempting to raise itself in the water by turning and bucking. Unpre-
pared for the situation, Randi was unseated before she was aware of
what was happening. She slipped from the saddle into the full force of
the river as her horse flailed and scrambled toward the shore.

"Lon!" Randi's single cry for help alerted Shawnee to her plight
as she attempted to swim toward shore. The weight of her drenched
clothes pulled her down, making it difficult for her to stay afloat. She
pulled in a deep breath and held it as she sank below the surface, trying to lift herself with her arms and legs. She continued to descend.
Her open eyes saw nothing but the water and the air bubbles rising
as air escaped from her lungs. Desperately, she tried even harder to
move her limbs to raise herself to the surface, but her strength rapidly
ran out. At the same time, she redoubled her effort to hold in the little
breath she had left.

Then, something gripped her tightly around her waist and began
lifting her. Distracted, she swallowed water and lost the breath she
had held. Wanting to breathe, her lungs pulled in a bit of water as she
was shoved above the surface, coughing and gasping for air.

Shawnee was beside her, holding her. "Hang on!" he shouted as
he swam hard for shore, dragging her with him. He held her close
to him, moving his arm lower and forcing her face above his to allow her to breathe and cough up water without swallowing more.
Slowly, swimming with one arm, he cut through the current and
progressed to the sediment of the submerged river bank. Using a
combination of swimming and walking, he got to a point at which
they were waist deep. He turned her and lifted her into his arms and
then walked out of the water as her gasps decreased and her breathing became less erratic.

Water drained from their clothing as Shawnee struggled up the
bank and onto grass. There, exhausted, he dropped to his knees and

placed Randi's body on the ground. Then he collapsed beside her. Both fought to catch their breath.

Randi rolled to her side and coughed up the last of the river left in her lungs and then fell on her back. Flashes of the incident ran through her mind, the uncontrollable fall into the water, the image of water in front of her as she sank, the arm gripping her and hauling her above the surface. A combination of tears and nervous laughter took her over, punctuated by coughing. She succumbed to it, making odd noises in a faint voice that were unintelligible even to herself. Then she lay there quietly, waiting for normal breathing to return.

8

SHAWNEE PROPPED HIMSELF ON AN elbow and stared at the woman on the ground beside him. Still breathing hard, he forced out, "Randi!"

She turned her head toward his voice and tried to focus on the cloudy image of his face. Blinking her eyes worked a little, but still there was the haziness. "Oh, God! Lon, what—how—?"

"Easy, now. You're safe. Got to get you dried off 'fore it starts cooling down." He pulled his feet under him and pushed himself to a standing position. Then he turned and walked quickly toward the tree line a few feet off the shore.

Randi, feeling the chill of the wet clothing against her body, sat up and wrapped her arms around her knees. She pulled herself into a ball and steeled herself against the approaching cold as the sun began to set. The events that had just transpired became clearer in her mind. That damn horse, afraid of heights, afraid of water. Got to get rid of him soon.

Burying herself in her thoughts to take her mind off the cold wetness, she did not hear Shawnee approach. She was a bit startled when he reached under her body and lifted her into his arms.

"Oh!" she said in surprise.

He started back toward the tree line, carrying her. "I got you. Got a fire going in a clearing back there. Got to get you warmed up." Hurrying through the trees, he entered a small open area which presented overhead clearance for the fire. He set her down close to the fire on a bed of branches and leaves cobbled together into a makeshift mattress.

"Get them wet clothes off and wrap yourself in the brush there to dry off. Stay close to the fire. I'm going to go round up the horses. I'll wait on the bank out there. Holler if'n you need something." He turned to leave.

"Lon."

He looked around.

"You're as wet as I am. You should dry off as well."

"That ain't a problem. I'll be fine. Just don't want you getting sick."

"Thanks for that, and for pulling me out."

He flashed a smile. "My pleasure, ma'am." He turned to walk away and stopped. "Look, I'm surely sorry I let you ride that nag into the river. Should a been me, and you on Gray."

Randi was taken with that. "How could you know?"

"I should a. I'm supposed to know stuff like that." He continued walking.

Randi took advantage of the privacy to peel her soaked clothes off and drop them in a pile beside her. Immediately, she wrapped herself in the leaves and brush Shawnee provided, finding it rough on her body but drying. She covered herself to her neck in the foliage and huddled there as the warmth of the fire abated the chill.

She wondered how he knew all these things? He must have had an interesting, eventful life to say the least. And he certainly was keeping his distance. My pleasure, ma'am, indeed!

———————

IT WAS DARK NOW. THE warmth thrown by the fire and the

scratchy caresses of the cut brush and leaves did their job. Randi, now fairly dry and devoid of the shivers, allowed her mind to drift from the concerns of things threatening her life. She looked around for Shawnee's presence. Right, he'd said he'd wait on the bank. He must have been freezing by now. "Lon." She hoped the call was loud enough for him to hear.

"Yes, ma'am." His voice betrayed the cold he experienced.

"Come in from there and get warm."

"I'm all right. Don't want to intrude."

"Lon, I'm warm and I'm not going to get sick. I'm worried that you will."

"You sure you're covered up?"

"It's like I had clothes on. Come on now."

Seconds passed and sounds could be heard coming from the trees. Shawnee led the three horses into the clearing. The bed rolls were opened out and draped across the backs of the horses. Shawnee had his arm through his coiled rope with the rope positioned on his shoulder. His face was pale, and his body shivered slightly. He said nothing and made an effort to refrain from looking at Randi.

"Lon, please," she said. "I'm as decent as I'm going to get. See to yourself. I trust you."

He pulled the rope from his shoulder and tied one end around a tree, then he pulled it taut and tied the other end on a low hanging branch across the clearing. It was placed near the fire, but not over it, effectively cutting the clearing in half with the fire on Randi's side. He stepped in close to Randi and picked up the pile of her wet clothes, never allowing his eyes to stray. Wringing the garments out, he opened them and hung them over the rope. This created a makeshift curtain across the camp, while at the same time becoming a drying line. He stepped behind the clothes, shielding himself from Randi's view, and removed his own wet outfit, placing them also over the rope.

Randi's ears picked up the sounds of him scratching together the extra brush that was strewn nearby. She caught glimpses of him covering himself with the stuff and then she looked away, trying to be as much a lady as he was a gentleman. She smiled, content that he was finally taking care of himself. Then exhaustion swept in to take control. She fell into a deep sleep.

THE RAYS OF THE MORNING sun peeked through Randi's fluttering eyes as she awakened the next morning. Memories of the night before, of almost drowning, and the events subsequent to that trauma, were vivid in her mind. Without thinking about her present state, she sat up, causing the leaves to fall away from her body. The chill that resulted brought to mind the fact that her clothes were hanging to dry and were not covering her. Quickly, she lay back down and scrambled to pull the leaves and brush over her.

Noises caused her to look around. Through the area of the drying line that had held her clothes, she saw him, fully dressed, crouched and rolling up the now dry bedrolls that had been opened out the night before.

She regarded him and could not get the thought out of her head that she would be forever grateful to the man for hauling her from a potentially watery grave. That translated to feelings for him that were better not pursued. At least, not yet. There was too much still to be done. She cleared her throat of the lingering night. "Good morning, Lon." As much as it was not her intent, her voice was a tad seductive.

He looked her way. "Morning, Randi. How're you feeling?"

"I don't know why, but I'm fine." There was a smile, a lilt to her speech that she could not explain.

"That's good. Reckon your clothes are dry when you're ready. Just let me know and I'll head out to the river."

"You don't have to do that. Just turn your back. I told you I trust you."

"Reckon you did. Just not sure I trust me."

"Lon, please. It's all right, really."

He stood up and turned his back to her, keeping his head still, facing away.

Quickly, she threw off the foliage and stood up to pull her clothes from the rope. As she hurriedly climbed into them, she noticed they were still damp. They would do, though, and the warmth of her body would dry them further. "You can turn around now," she said as she pulled her boots on.

He looked around and smiled, then he continued packing up the camp. "Hungry?"

"Starving."

"We got the last of the venison." He dug the packets from the packhorse's stores. "Little damp but it's eatable."

They shared the meat while crouching close to each other.

"I'm curious about something," he said.

"What's that?"

"Well, while I was cleaning the guns, making sure they work after getting soaked, I noticed that piece you carry. It's pretty and all, but it's kind of puny, ain't it? Thirty-eight's a small caliber."

Randi smiled at his interest. "I wanted something with a light recoil. And I have short thumbs. It's hard for me to cock a full size pistol with one hand. Mine doesn't need to be cocked, so it fits both requirements."

Shawnee nodded. "Yeah, I noticed that. Surely makes sense."

"There's something I'm curious about. Where did you learn to swim like that?"

"My pa learned me. Thought it'd come in handy sometime. Reckon he was right."

She smiled. "He certainly was."

They finished eating and continued packing for the trail.

"I figure we'll be in Santa Fe by noon or so." He completed saddling Gray as he spoke.

They mounted and moved out of the woods. Riding across rocky ground, they came to the mouth of the Pecos River and followed it south. Shawnee's estimate proved true as they came upon the outskirts of Santa Fe at approximately noon.

At the crest of a hill not far out, they drew rein and viewed the vast landscape that contained the city.

Resting in a large open area between two mountainous regions, Santa Fe contained several well-traveled streets with many buildings lining both sides. The basic architecture was Spanish in origin, with older structures being adobe and newer ones of wood construction. In the outlying sections, various businesses and factories occupied large quarters while, still farther out, homes and a few farms dotted around.

"We need to keep this as quiet as possible," Randi said. "We should make camp in a secluded spot. I'll go in and meet with the governor and bring him to you. The rest is up to you."

"Thanks for seeing this through. I know it ain't been easy for you, likely more'n you bargained for."

"I'm just doing my job, Lon. Nothing more or less." Her expression was serious.

"Yeah, well, you can tell yourself that, but I'm leaning toward there's more to it." He flashed a knowing smile.

She shook her head, not wanting to let on yet. Too much to do. "I have no idea what you're talking about. Come on, let's find that campsite."

AFTER ACCOMPANYING SHAWNEE TO A dense ponderosa
pine forest outside Santa Fe, Randi committed its location to memory
and proceeded into the city, taking her carpetbag with her. Certain
that none of her clothes, having been soaked in the waters of the Rio
Grande, were in presentable enough condition to be acceptable for a
meeting with Governor Wallace, she sought out a clothier at which
she purchased a new outfit. All of her worn clothing was stuffed into
the bag. She left her horse at a nearby stable. Now clad in a fitted burgundy dress and matching hat, she learned the location of the Palace
of the Governors and headed there in a hired carriage.

The Palace, the oldest continuously occupied building in the United States, was constructed early in the seventeenth century to house
the first Spanish governor of New Mexico. It was a long, one story
adobe affair, the length of a city block, on Palace Avenue between
Lincoln and Washington Avenues in the heart of the city. Large log
posts, supporting the roof, jutted out from the facade. Massive wood
pillars held the long eave covering the walkway in place.

Randi was impressed by the simple but majestic beauty of the
building as the carriage driver stopped the conveyance at the entrance.
Above the doorway, twin flagpoles rose on the roof, one bearing the
flag of the United States, the other flying the flag of New Mexico. Familiar with the location, the driver directed Randi to the governor's
office inside.

She stood at the door marked Gov. Lew Wallace and knocked
gently. Without waiting for permission, she entered. Her guise of a
reporter had to start right now if it was to be believed and, as a reporter, she needed to be assertive, but not aggressive.

She stepped into an ornate outer office consisting of several chairs
and a couch bound in matching leather. The chairs were placed along

the wall in waiting room fashion while the couch resided against the opposite wall. Each wall was decorated with paintings of outdoor scenes, probably depicting locations within New Mexico. In front of her, a mahogany desk was occupied by a well-dressed man in his late twenties, stocky, with a round face and wavy black hair. The identification plate on the desk stated, George Hardrick. Randi guessed, as she approached, that this was the governor's secretary or receptionist. He looked up when she reached the desk.

"Good day to you, ma'am." His voice was deep and resonant. "May I help you?"

"My name is Randi Swayze. I'm a reporter working on a series of articles about the work of territorial governors. May I see Governor Wallace?"

"Do you have an appointment?"

"I do not. I just arrived in Santa Fe and was hoping to interview the governor before moving on to Arizona. I'm under a deadline to submit my work."

"I'm sorry, ma'am, but Governor Wallace sees no one without an appointment."

"I quite understand that, but, perhaps, if you asked him, he might relent and see me. It will only take a few minutes of his time and will mean so much to me. I have a lot riding on the success of this article."

The smile accompanying her words tended to soften his resolve.

"Well...."

"Please. You don't know how difficult it is for a woman to get ahead in the journalistic world. This would go a long way toward validating my standing as a reporter." Her smile broadened and, at the same time, projected supplication.

He hesitated. "I'm... not supposed to...." His words trailed off as he appeared to reconsider.

She pressed on. "Please, I implore you. If you could simply ask him. If he refuses, I'll leave and cause you no more distress."

He scrunched his face, indicating contemplation. She tried to turn her expression into an illustration of her plea. He rose. "Wait here," he said quietly, with uncertainty.

"And please tell him my name. Randi Swayze. He might be familiar with my work."

She allowed her body to relax as he turned to knock on the door to the governor's private office.

A man's voice inside allowed entry. He quickly stepped in and closed the door behind him. Several seconds later, he emerged. "The governor will see you."

Randi gushed a thank you and moved to the open doorway. As she stepped inside the room, as ornately decorated as was the outer office, the governor, seated at the massive, intricately carved desk, looked up.

Wallace was an imposing figure with a full, well-trimmed mustache and Van Dyke beard that almost completely covered his mouth. Perched on his nose was a pair of pince-nez eyeglasses. He had a full head of dark hair, parted on the side, with several strands hanging across the side of his forehead. He wore a well-tailored suit. His expression was stern, and he seemed agitated.

"Come in, Miss Swayze, close the door."

Randi did as instructed and then continued toward the desk as Wallace rose to greet her. They shook hands.

"It's an honor to meet you, sir."

"Thank you." He gestured to one of the two upholstered chairs that faced the desk. "Please, sit down."

She took a seat, sitting straight-backed, primly. He occupied the adjacent chair, facing her.

"I hoped you would recognize my name." She smiled.

"Yes, from the telegram you sent, and Mister Pinkerton mentioned you as the agent he would assign to the case. What he did not tell me is that you are this charming."

"Thank you, sir, but we should get right to business. To maintain my cover, I passed myself off to your secretary as a reporter and said I only needed a few minutes with you. I don't want to raise questions."

"Very well. You can speak freely here."

"Alonzo Pearce is waiting at a campsite just outside the city. I thought it best to keep him hidden."

"I agree." Wallace leaned forward in the chair, showing interest. "We need to keep this entire operation under wraps. I assume he's agreed to my proposal?"

"He's indicated a willingness to listen to your proposal. I'm not certain he's totally convinced. He tends to be a little cryptic at times."

"Well, then, I'll need to convince him so we can move forward."

"I can take you to him."

Wallace leaned back, appearing satisfied. "Excellent. We should leave separately. You first. The government corral is a short walk from here. I'll meet you there in ten minutes. There is someone I want to accompany us."

Randi was becoming steadily more concerned. "I believe he'd want to meet with you alone, Governor. The presence of a stranger might make him suspicious."

Wallace raised a hand to calm her. "Don't worry. This man is not a stranger to him. I'm sure he'll know Marshal Driskill."

9

THE LIGHT KNOCK ON HIS office door pulled Phin Driskill's attention away from the report he tried to finish. It was late in the day, and he was hungry, and the last thing he needed right now was another interruption.

"What?" He said it loud enough to be heard through the door. His call revealed his distress with the path his job in general and this document in particular was on.

In response to his question, the door opened and George Hardrick leaned in. "Good day, Marshal. Governor Wallace would like to see you."

Driskill studied the man, delaying his reply a few seconds. Hardrick stepped farther inside. Driskill breathed a sigh. "All right, tell him I'll be along directly."

"You might want to rethink that, Mister Driskill. He was pretty emphatic about bringing you now."

Driskill shrugged. He pulled in and let out a loud breath. "All right, let's go now." There was resignation in his voice.

He rose and rounded the desk in a few steps. Hardrick swung the door open wider to allow Driskill to fit past him and then closed the door. Driskill was already a few steps ahead of him, walking briskly through the corridor, as the young man fell in behind.

Driskill was tall and stocky with a full, well-trimmed gray beard. His bushy head of hair had been slicked back in an attempt to appear neat. The position of Chief Territorial Marshal put him in contact with a lot of well-placed people, and it didn't do for his appearance to be inappropriate. He was still uncomfortable in this suit, with its starched collar and neck-tie, but it was the accepted dress around here. He preferred trail clothes.

It was a little more than a year now since he'd been recruited for this job. Having worked as a deputy sheriff, then a sheriff, at no higher than the county level, his manner of dress was much less formal than that required here.

No matter. Likely won't last much longer anyhow. He'd been next to useless in breaking up this gang of raiders that ran roughshod over the territory. Every time he'd thought he had them in a bind, they'd slipped through his fingers. The governor was likely summoning him now to tell him to pack up and move on.

Throughout the walk to the governor's office, Hardrick never caught up with Driskill. He was not as tall as the marshal and, short of running, was unable to match his pace. Driskill stopped at the outer office door and waited for Hardrick to reach him.

Breathlessly, Hardrick arrived and opened the door. "I'll tell him you're here."

Driskill followed him into the office.

Hardrick tapped on the inner door, opened it, and stuck his head inside. "Marshal Driskill, sir," he said past the door. He turned then and gestured to Driskill to proceed inside. As the marshal passed him, he closed the door, remaining outside.

Driskill stopped in the center of the room. Wallace rounded his desk and met him half way.

"Thanks for coming quickly, Chief. We've got to take a little trip. A friend of yours is in town."

Driskill appeared puzzled. The governor typically did not hide his gist. When Wallace raised his finger to his lips to indicate quiet, though, Driskill picked up the existence of a double meaning and nodded comprehension.

IN A SECLUDED CORNER OF the vast area known as the government corral, Randi stood waiting somewhat impatiently. Her carpetbag was on the ground nearby. This area consisted of a central courtyard surrounded by stables housing horses and equipment used by officials of the territorial government.

"Ten minutes," he said. That must have passed a while ago. What was keeping him? And who was this third person he insisted on bringing?

Agitated, she began to pace. With her back turned to the gate that allowed admission from Washington Avenue, she heard the entry of two people. She turned to face them as Wallace and another man approached quietly.

"Thank you for waiting, Miss Swayze," Wallace said. "Allow me to introduce Chief Territorial Marshal Driskill. It was his recommendation that prompted me to seek out Mister Pearce."

"Ma'am." Driskill tipped his hat.

Randi nodded. "How do you do, Marshal. I hope this won't upset Mister Pearce's readiness to listen."

"It might take some nudging, but I reckon he'll remember me."

Randi was not convinced. "I hope so. If you had any idea what we've gone through to get here, you'd be as concerned as I am about anything that might disrupt this."

"I'm sure you've had your difficulties, Miss Swayze," Wallace told her, not unkindly. "However, I really *do* think Marshal Driskill's presence will help convince him."

"I'll leave that up to you, Governor," Randi said. "In any event, we should get started before it gets too dark to find the camp."

"I'll get a buggy hitched up," Driskill said as he moved into the corral.

A few minutes later, a one horse buggy left the corral with Driskill driving and Randi guiding. They took an indirect route out of the city, keeping to more deserted streets. The governor, in the back seat, was obscured by the structure of the carriage, making it difficult to discern his identity. Once clear of the streets and into the countryside, Driskill whipped up the horse to reach the destination before dark.

Dusk rolled in as they neared the ponderosa forest, but enough light remained for Randi to direct them to the clearing where the camp was set up.

"Stop here," she said.

Driskill pulled rein at the tree line. They exited the buggy, and Randi led them into the woods, then on into the clearing that hosted the camp. There was no sign of Shawnee, although the fire in the center flourished as if it had been recently tended.

"That's far enough." Shawnee's voice sounded from the woods in front of them.

They stopped not far from the fire. Randi remained behind the two men. Shawnee stepped from behind a tree with his sidearm drawn and leveled. He moved toward them, watching them carefully.

"Howdy, Shawnee," Driskill said. "Been a spell since Bodeen."

Shawnee studied the man for a few seconds before speaking. "Yeah, Driskill, ain't it? Deputy sheriff back then."

"It's chief marshal now, but, yeah, you got it right."

"What're you doing here?"

"I'm the one told the governor about you, about you being the *hombre* could pull this off if anyone can. This is Governor Wallace, here."

Shawnee nodded but seemed unimpressed. "Governor."

Wallace stepped forward. "I'll get right to the point, Mister Pearce. I'm sure Miss Swayze has explained the proposition I have for you. I assume by your presence here that you've at least considered it. Just to be clear, I'm asking you to join the outlaw organization that has been running rampant here. If you can locate their hideout and bring them down, I'm prepared to issue an order of amnesty that wipes out the offenses of which you've been accused. You would be a free man from that point on."

Shawnee lowered his revolver along his leg, pointed at the ground. "What if I ain't able to bring 'em down?"

"In that case, I'm sorry to say that you probably won't not survive the attempt."

"Reckon that's how I'd cipher it, too." Shawnee thought for a second. "Say, how's this amnesty thing work anyhow? Seems I recollect reading about that Billy Bonney *hombre* getting amnesty, but he still wound up on the short end."

"Bonney didn't follow the rules. He failed to stay on the right side of the law. Amnesty will only wipe out your previous offenses. If you break the law after the order is issued, you're still subject to arrest and trial for that offense. If you're convicted, you will face the prescribed punishment. From all I've heard about you, I believe you to be smarter and of better character than Bonney."

Shawnee studied Wallace closely for a few seconds, then placed his gun back in its holster. "I need to ponder on that a spell." He walked past the group and into the forest.

Wallace turned to Randi. "Miss Swayze, you've spent time with him. Is he taking this seriously?"

"He is, Governor. I've seen it before. That just seems to be the way he thinks things through."

"Very well. In the meantime, then, when can I expect the bill for your services?"

"I'm merely an employee, sir. The bill will come from Pinkerton headquarters after I submit my final report. I don't know the timing of it."

"I must tell you, Miss Swayze, based on what you've accomplished here, you cannot be termed *merely* anything. Not in the least."

"Thank you." She made no attempt to hide the fact that she was flattered by the remark.

Shawnee spoke from inside the tree line. "I do this, it's got to be my way or it won't work." He stepped back into the clearing and stopped in front of Wallace and Driskill. "For me to get into that bunch, they got to believe I'm as good at outlawing as they be, maybe better, so they come looking for me. That's the only way they'll buy this."

"You saying you're going to raid in their back yard?" Driskill asked.

"That's about the size of it."

"What's to stop 'em from just killing you, get rid of the competition?"

"Nothing. Chance I got to take."

"I'm not sure I'm comfortable with what you're proposing," the governor said. "Innocent people could get hurt, or at least, lose their property."

"Did you reckon this'd be a picnic? I just show up and say I want to join 'em, and they say come on in and welcome? You even know where their hideout is? No, they got to come for me. Far as anything I take, I'll keep it hid to give back when this is over. And I ain't looking to hurt nobody. I'll make sure of that."

Deep in thought, Wallace did not reply. Driskill leaned close to him. A whispered discussion followed.

"Look, Governor," Shawnee said, staring straight at the man, "I got a lot of respect for you, what you done in the war and all, but you come to me with this, I didn't come to you. Every minute I'm here, I'm sticking my neck way out. So, either we do this my way, or we don't do it at all, and I'll just head on back to Mexico now. But I ain't standing here all night hashing it out with you. I done my deciding. Time you done yours."

Wallace studied Shawnee intensely for several seconds. "You are absolutely correct, Mister Pearce. I've made my decision as well. You have carte blanche regarding this operation."

"Come again?"

"How you conduct this is completely up to you. Short of killing or wounding innocent bystanders, I authorize your every action. And I'm prepared to accept the consequences if this fails."

Shawnee extended his hand. "Reckon I am, as well."

They shook.

Wallace turned to Driskill. "Chief, will you give Mister Pearce the information he needs?"

"Yes, sir."

"Mister Pearce, whether this succeeds or not, you have my gratitude. When you've completed this, I will issue your order of amnesty. Good luck and God speed." Wallace stepped back and turned to leave, stopping next to Randi. "Miss Swayze?"

"I'll be along directly, Governor," Randi said.

The governor stepped away to return to the buggy.

Driskill moved closer to Shawnee.

"So I got you to thank for getting me into this, eh?" Shawnee said.

"Don't thank me yet. I might've caused you more harm than good."

"Yeah, we'll see about that. So, what can you tell me about these *hombres*?"

"First off, they been operating around Alburkurk and Valencia, spreading out from there. They hit everything, coaches, mine payrolls, banks, everything." There was frustration in Driskill's voice. "I can't count how many times I laid traps for 'em, and they slipped right through. It's like they already knew about 'em. I'd swear they got somebody in Santa Fe tipping 'em off. Ain't said nothing to the governor about it 'cause I can't prove it, but I sure as hell believe it."

"Sounds about right. Any idea who's running the outfit?"

"Naw! Not a one. Whoever he is, he's smart as a whip the way he sets up his raids. Uses diversions and all. That's another reason I think he's getting inside information. And he ain't afraid to kill the folks gets in his way."

"I'll keep that in mind."

"Something else to keep in mind. I'm assigning one of my deputies to shadow you just in case you get in a bind. He won't get in your way, but he'll be around if you need him."

Shawnee raised a hand in a halting gesture. "Now, hold on there. Maybe that ain't such a good idea. I don't want him tipping my hand."

"He won't. You won't even know he's around. Look, you had my back in Bodeen. Least I can do is return the favor."

"That's up to you. Where was the last raid?"

"Alburkurk. They hit a bank there."

"Then I reckon I'll head for Alburkurk come sun-up."

Driskill extended his hand. "Good luck and take care."

They shook hands. Driskill turned and started back toward the buggy, coming to Randi.

"I'll be right there," she said as he passed her. She moved closer to Shawnee.

"Thanks for sticking your neck out like you done," he said. "Reckon you'll be heading out now your job's done."

Randi smiled. "Actually, no. I'm going to take a little time off right here in Santa Fe."

"Well, that's interesting. Any reason for staying here?"

She stepped to within an inch of him. Her hand went to his arm and rested there. Initially, he tensed at her touch, then he relaxed. She wanted desperately to kiss him, to reveal her feelings for him. She hesitated as she turned it over in her mind, finally deciding against it. Not the time. "I've had enough traveling for a while," she said to fill the void. Then she turned and left quickly. "I need to watch a sunset or two."

10

"TIME TO GET GOING, GRAY. We got us a job of work to do." Shawnee stepped into the stirrup and pulled himself into the saddle as Gray turned to exit the forest. The morning sun was cresting over the hills and forcing its rays through the pine trees.

Shawnee had come off a restless night concentrating on formulating a plan to disrupt the outlaws' raiding pattern and become conspicuous. Still distracted by Randi's cryptic actions the previous evening, he'd found it necessary to push himself back to setting the steps required to put this ruse in motion.

Scouting the area for a secure hideout was necessary so he could squirrel away whatever loot he gathered. Each incident would be noted in detail so the proceeds could be returned to the rightful owners when this operation was done. Meanwhile, specific information needed to be gathered in the towns Driskill had mentioned. Albuquerque first, then Valencia. These facts would indicate the level of importance and the order in which his attacks would take place. They had to be important enough to get the outlaws' attention.

Well into the early morning hours, in a quandary after a final reflection on Randi's apparent feelings toward him, he finally drifted off into a light sleep. That only lasted a short time, annulled by the breaking light of dawn.

After a hurried meal, he broke camp and saddled Gray. Heading southwest, he covered close to seventy miles of hill country and dense forests that led to the outskirts of Albuquerque in three days of sustained riding. Stopping only to rest and feed Gray and to rest himself and consume trail rations, he rode from dawn to dark. His camps were makeshift and cold, allowing him to attract little to no attention. This would be his practice until he was ready to make his presence known.

As he crested a hill that led to what he believed to be the main road to Albuquerque, the sound of gunfire caused him to pull up sharply. Instinctively, he checked around to be certain he was not the target of the shots. They were that close. Satisfied, he advanced carefully around some bushes and observed a stagecoach in the middle of the road. It was at a standstill, obstructed by three horsemen with side arms drawn. The driver held the reins tight on the seat while the man next to him, likely the guard, was hunched over, holding his left arm.

Shawnee made a fast cipher of what had just happened. The three raiders threw down on the coach, intending to rob it. The guard tried to fight back and got shot for his trouble. Shawnee was not ready to get into this right now, still in the planning stages, but what the hell, no time like the present. He had a surprise on his side. Might as well use it.

He pulled his revolver and drew a bead on the closest rider. The single shot hit the man, doubling him over in the saddle. He urged his horse up to speed and rode off behind the coach.

As the two remaining intruders turned to address the origin of the shot, Shawnee's advance down the slope toward them was already in progress. He kept his fire high to avoid hitting the men on the coach but low enough to make the outlaws think twice about continuing to fight. His three shots came between the two, each fired by the raiders. None were hits, but Shawnee's were closer to their mark. His aggression softened their resolve. As he reached the road level, they pulled their mounts around and set out in the direction from which the coach had come. Both rode away at a gallop as Shawnee pulled up at the coach and fired his last shot after them.

Immediately, he began ejecting the empties from his gun and replacing them with live rounds. He kept the weapon in hand.

"Whooee!" the mustached driver shouted gleefully. "Stranger, you surely showed up in the nick o' time. Them three owlhoots had us cold, me with my hands full of horseflesh and Lou, here, taking a bullet."

"Glad to oblige," Shawnee said simply. He moved Gray close to the coach and examined the guard's wound. "Little more'n a scratch. You'll be all right."

As he spoke, he glanced at the roof of the coach, at the strongbox lashed behind the driver. "That an express box you got there?"

"Yep," the driver said readily. "That's what they was after."

Shawnee backed Gray up a little. "Now, friend, you just seen me reload this piece, so I'd advise you to think hard on what your next move'll be." He raised the revolver and cocked it. "What you need to do is throw that box down and whip that team up, and get your friend to a sawbones right quick. You do that, and nothing'll happen to you." He tried hard to sound like a convincing lawbreaker.

The driver took a second to digest what he just heard, then voiced his anger, "Son-of-a-bitch!" He made an awkward move indicating his intention to resist.

"Uh-uh," Shawnee said, "think hard."

The man dropped his move. "Aw, shit!" Taking the reins in one hand, he reached behind him and released the leather lash on the box.

With a push of his hand, he upended it and sent it over the side of the coach to the ground. It landed with a metallic thud.

Shawnee smiled. "Thanks, friend, you done the right thing. Now get gone."

Before Shawnee's statement was finished, the driver, cursing, set the six-in-hand team in motion, leaving the scene in a hurry. Shawnee dismounted and went to the strongbox, stooping and hefting it—heavy enough to call for a hideout close by. He reckoned this would become his first task, finding a secure retreat capable of sheltering this and any other valuables he took during this undertaking.

He lifted the box and carried it to where Gray stood. He tied it to the blanket roll behind his saddle. Mounting, he rode slowly back up the slope to the top of the hill as the box shifted precariously. From there, the search began.

———————

AFTER SEVERAL HOURS OF SCOURING heavily wooded areas in the higher elevations to the east, he came upon an abandoned mineshaft dug into the side of a hill. This deserted region was shielded by a dense ponderosa pine forest that stretched for miles around. The stumps of many trees long ago cut down for access ringed the outside of the shaft, indicating activity from years past. Now, it stood as a monument to a more productive time.

Shawnee and Gray approached. The timber frame that formed the rectangular opening came into view. Shawnee's sense of foreboding grew at the sight of the decaying condition of the wood. He pulled Gray up a few yards away and dismounted. Carefully, he moved closer, stopping at the entrance to examine the structure. A stout shove on the timbers shook small granules of earth loose that showered down on his hat and shoulders. The structure held, telling him the beams were still basically sound. They looked worse than they were. He brushed the dirt from his clothes. Tentatively, he stepped across the threshold and struck a match across his chaps to light the inside.

The walls and ceiling of the short tunnel were bare earth-shored up by additional timber supports. As the match flickered, Shawnee gauged the length to be about twelve feet and the height about eight feet. He stepped farther in to see the end still showing marks where a pick had dislodged chunks of dirt. Some of those pieces lay in a haphazard array on the floor. A lone, rusting pick-ax lay beside them.

He reckoned that whoever last worked this mine had decided it was a bust and abandoned it, leaving partially finished work and the tool behind.

Satisfied this would make an acceptable hiding place, he shook out the match as the flame closed on his fingers. He turned for the exit. Walking outside, he released the strongbox from its mooring on Gray's back and carted it into the shaft. He returned to Gray and found paper and pencil in his saddlebag. Using the surface of the saddle seat, he scribbled the date and location of the stagecoach robbery and placed the note into the seam between the top and bottom of the box. When he finished, he remounted and directed Gray back into the forest.

———————

THE LIGHTS OF ALBUQUERQUE BURNED brightly as night rolled in. Shawnee and Gray descended a hill that led to the beginnings of the town. It was some time now since he was in a town of this size, or any town for that matter. For him, these places usually meant the possibility of being recognized. That usually generated some attempt to arrest him or at least purse him. This time, he didn't care. If he were identified, that would simply advertise that he was in the area. While this was not his intention in coming here, he would not discount its importance. Word needed to get back to the leader of the raiders quickly that he was here and was a threat. Any means of making that happen were acceptable.

He rode tonight on a scouting mission. He needed information regarding vulnerable, well-paying situations if he was to crowd this bunch. Listening to saloon conversations and roaming the streets should give him enough fodder to plan his next attacks.

Albuquerque was a sprawling, growing community of mainly wood-frame buildings. None of the Mexican architecture that dominated Santa Fe existed here. A much younger town, its American founders influenced its architecture and built it accordingly.

Shawnee rode slowly along Railroad Avenue toward the activity surrounding a group of hotels and their adjoining businesses, saloons, restaurants, and dance halls. He directed Gray to the hitch rail in front of a particularly active drinking establishment and dismounted.

Light, noise, and something resembling music came from inside. He expected he would likely pick up something here.

As he tied off Gray's reins, he glanced around to memorize the lay of the area as he usually did in a strange town, making note of dark alleys and escape routes. This was standard practice for him. He had to constantly plan ahead in case he was recognized and was required to make a fast getaway.

Satisfied, he mounted the boardwalk and pushed through the batwings into a chaotic scene of raucous men, ladies of the evening, and copious amounts of liquor flowing readily. The long bar stood on the right, supporting a line of men two-deep in various stages of drunkenness, clamoring for drinks while hanging onto scantily clad women bargaining for the sale of their bodies. To his left, a group of erratically placed tables, some with four chairs, some with more, were occupied by drinkers and their tainted doves engaging in everything from conversation to the early phases of that which the rooms upstairs existed to conclude.

In the corner behind the tables, a young man in a crisp suit, his back to the activities, played a familiar refrain on a remarkably well-tuned upright piano.

Shawnee moved to the near end of the bar and elbowed his way into a spot that sandwiched him between the wall and a cowpoke whose arms, locked into the hump on the bar, were the only things holding him upright. The barkeep, a pudgy fellow with a round, balding head and a soiled white shirt, closed in on him and shouted over the din to ask Shawnee's preference.

"Bourbon." Shawnee had to equal the barman's volume to be heard.

The man moved quickly down the bar and returned with a large shot glass and an unlabeled bottle. He poured the drink.

"Two bits."

Shawnee fished a coin from his shirt pocket and placed it on the bar as the bartender studied him. The usual question was about to be asked.

"Say, ain't I seen you in here before? You look familiar."

Shawnee grinned. "Yeah, I get that a lot. I got one of them faces. Look like a lot of folks. Never been here before."

The man shrugged and picked up the coins. "Enjoy your evening."

Shawnee lifted the drink and tossed it down. "Thanks." The stuff burned his throat. Uncertain if it was even bourbon, but certain it wasn't worth the price, he moved away from the bar and began to circulate through the tables, appearing to search for a seat while straining his ears to gather available information from the occupants. His progress through gained nothing useful.

He closed on a table from which an overweight man in a suit and tie rose with a woman hanging onto him. They staggered to the stair-case at the back wall. As they wrapped their arms around each other, they made a valiant attempt to navigate the steps without tripping, giggling all the way. Shawnee moved quickly to the table and assumed ownership by sitting down.

Immediately, a young woman sauntered to his side to ask what he would have. He noted that the over-application of cheap makeup and the short, low-cut black dress made her less attractive.

"Bourbon." He might as well stick with the same poison.

"Want company with that?" she asked boldly.

He flashed a forced smile. "No offense, ma'am. I'm drinking alone tonight."

She shrugged. "Your choice." She moved away.

He glanced around, keeping his ears sharp as he observed two stocky men at a nearby table. They leaned in close and engaged in a private discussion.

Dressed in plaid wool coats that bore dust in their colors, their appearance indicated to Shawnee that they worked hard, maybe as teamsters. He strained to hear their exchange and gathered they drove and guarded for a local express company. The conversation told him they were driving in the morning between Albuquerque and Valencia to deliver a payroll. They planned to leave shortly after sunup. The talk concluded as both finished their beers and got up to leave.

Shawnee waited a second as they threaded their way through the tables. As he rose, the saloon girl returned with his drink.

"Four bits," she said as she handed him the glass.

He dug out the fee and handed it to her but did not take the glass. "Two for the drink, the other two for the delivery, huh?" he said absently. "Have one on me." He dropped the coins into her hand and brushed past her.

She shrugged and, without hesitation, tossed the liquor back in one swallow.

Pushing through the batwings, Shawnee glanced up and down the street for the two men. Based on what he'd heard inside, he began to form a plan in his head. He needed to follow them for any further information he could gather before morning.

He stayed close enough to keep them in sight but far enough back to avoid being seen. Adept at this from previous practice, he tailed them through a few streets to one of the less expensive hotels off Railroad Avenue. They entered the establishment, ending his ability to shadow them undetected. He turned back toward the main street to see what other information he could turn up.

As he approached the hitch rail where Gray stood among a few others mounts, his attention was drawn across the street. The woman entering the hotel there was tall, like Randi. Light from the street lamps and from inside the inn showed that same burgundy dress and hat Randi wore at the meeting with the governor.

The woman disappeared inside. Shawnee stopped in the middle of the street. She surely looked like Randi. What the hell was she doing here? His hand went to the back of his neck in that gesture of confusion as he pondered on her sudden decision to remain in Santa Fe. He shook his head.

Seconds later, he decided this was not the time or the place to get involved with unraveling her intentions. He moved on to Gray and mounted. For now, he would be satisfied with the information about the mine payroll. He would return later to pursue other ventures, including Randi. Pulling Gray around, he headed up a side street in search of a secluded place nearby to spend the night.

11

JUST AFTER SUN-UP, A BUCKBOARD drawn by a trotting two-horse hitch moved along the main road out of Albuquerque heading south. Aboard, the two men Shawnee had observed in the saloon the prior night sat on the thick board that served as a seat. The driver kept the team at a constant speed while the guard, shotgun across his lap, scanned the country ahead and occasionally glanced to the rear.

Ahead about a quarter mile, Shawnee, seated on Gray, peeked out from his position behind thick bushes on the side of the trail. The sight of the wagon and the speed of its movement told him this was what he was here for. He dismounted quickly and knelt alongside Gray's left front leg. His hand went to the horse's leg just below the knee and folded the leg up to an angle, effectively shifting Gray's weight to the other three hooves. "Hold that, Gray, hold that."

The horse obeyed the command as Shawnee rose, maintaining the three-legged stance. Shawnee stepped in front of Gray and tugged gently on the reins, moving out of the brush. "Hold that, son."

In order to follow and still comply with the order, Gray limped, keeping the raised hoof off the ground. They slowly entered the narrow trail and stopped in the center. "Hold that." Shawnee had planned this as a distraction to cause the two men to drop their guard.

The buckboard approached at a constant speed until it was only yards away. The driver, likely realizing there was no room to go around the encumbrance before him, hauled back on the reins and pulled the team to a chaotic halt.

In truth, Shawnee chose this spot for that exact result. Much better than pouncing on them and chancing a gun battle or chasing them and wearing himself and Gray out. This way, he had them without a struggle before they ciphered what he'd done.

"Hey," the driver called. "Get out of the way."

In response, Shawnee said nothing as he turned to Gray, bent down, and straightened the horse's leg. He rose and mounted. As his leg cleared the saddle, his hand lifted the revolver from its holster. Once seated, he brought the gun into clear sight and cocked it.

"What the hell—" the driver said as the guard moved to cock the shotgun hammers.

"Don't," Shawnee told him.

The guard froze, his thumb still on the hammers.

"This is just what it looks like," Shawnee said. "I'm taking that express box. Now, toss your guns in the bushes."

The two men hesitated.

"Do it."

The guard heaved the shotgun into the bushes to his left while the driver pitched his side arm away to his right.

"All of them."

The guard cursed under his breath and reached out his revolver, tossing it to join the shotgun.

"Guard, get hold of that box and bring it here."

The man jumped down from the seat and reached into the wagon's bed. Due to the awkward angle, he lifted the metal box with some effort to clear the sideboard.

"Don't do nothing but what I tell you," Shawnee said. "I ain't looking to shoot nobody. Bring it here."

The guard carried the box by its handles and walked to where Gray stood.

"Tie it off behind me. Make sure it's tight."

"Son of a bitch." The man lifted the box to the blanket roll behind the saddle seat and used the tie-downs to lash it in place. Shawnee reached behind and tested the stability of the box.

"Get back up on the wagon."

The guard returned to his seat.

Shawnee directed Gray to the side of the road, making room for the wagon. "Now, driver, you whip up that team and get out of here. Don't stop till you wear 'em out."

With a shout at the horses, the driver slapped the reins across their backs. The team burst into a gallop, hauling the buckboard away in a cloud of trail dust.

Shawnee watched for a few seconds to be certain they had kept going. Then he turned Gray into the bushes and headed east.

———————————

SEVERAL DAYS LATER, SHAWNEE'S ENTRY into Valencia drew no attention. Though the town had been through various versions over the last two hundred years, this was his first visit there.

Beginning as a land grant in the seventeenth century, it grew and fell several times due to minor wars and floods from the nearby Rio Grande. It stood now as a town combining Mexican and American-influenced architecture. Most buildings were new, but a few were rebuilds of older structures that had been salvaged from one catastrophe or another.

Shawnee rode the main street, taking in this rich expression of history. At the half way point, he stopped Gray at a hitch rail. He looked around to familiarize himself with the lay of the land and any escape routes that existed. This time, however, his gaze lingered, digesting individuals' faces and how they carried themselves.

Several men stood nearby, their attention focused on the facade of a bank. To the casual eye, they merely loitered. To Shawnee, however, their posture, their edginess, was apparent. They glanced around just a tad too much. Combined with the fact that he recognized a couple of their faces from wanted posters that, at one time or another, had appeared next to his own, Shawnee anticipated a robbery in the offing.

A plan came together in his mind. If it worked, he'd have another job under his belt and thwarting these *hombres'* intentions. A double coup. Pulling Gray's reins, he quickly headed into an alley beside the bank. Following it to the other end, he dismounted and ground-tied Gray.

The back wall of the bank building had a door and one window. Discounting the door as too dangerous, he approached the window carefully and checked the view inside through the pane. Empty. It looked to be an office. He tested the sash. Locked. A glance told him the swivel lock was reachable from outside. He lifted the gun belt higher on his hip to access his pants pocket and fished out a small fold-out pocket knife. The blade was thin enough to fit between the upper and lower sashes and to throw the lock into the open position. Replacing the knife, he lifted the lower sash and climbed in.

The office was small and sparsely furnished. A plain wood desk and chair were positioned directly in front of the window. To Shawnee's right, a door seemed to separate the office from the bank's business area. He went quickly to the door, drawing his revolver as he moved. Stopping for a second to listen for sounds on the other side that might indicate a robbery in progress, he concluded that the noise was only normal business.

Reassured there was still time to pull this off, he lowered the pistol to a position perpendicular to the floor along his leg so it wouldn't be readily noticed. He carefully opened the door.

The business floor of the bank took up the entire front of the building. A single teller sat in a wire cage to the left. Behind him, the small steel vault door was open. Four customers stood in line at the opening in the cage, their backs to the double front door.

As Shawnee stepped unnoticed onto the business floor, he raised the gun and moved quickly to the front door, scanning it to locate the position of the lock. At the same time, the lead customer turned away from the teller's cage and approached the door. Shawnee locked the door and turned to stand in the customer's way. "Nobody move. This is a holdup."

The customer froze, as did the other three. The teller peered around them to take this in. Shawnee moved forward, waving the revolver to direct the man in front of him to the side. "All of you, up against the wall."

The customers obeyed as Shawnee went quickly to the cage.

"Put the loose money in a sack and hand it here," he said as he reached the cage opening.

The teller did as he was told, fumbling for a sack and then stuffing bills and coins from the vault into it.

Shawnee watched until the sack was full. "That'll do," he said, keeping his gun trained on the customers. "Give it here."

The teller pushed the sack through the small opening. Shawnee grabbed it and stepped back. "Stay put and nobody gets hurt." He moved quickly through the doorway into the office and kicked the door shut. Holstering the gun, he threw the door lock and went directly to the open window. A quick climb put him outside. He took up Gray's reins and swung smoothly into the saddle. He wondered briefly what the reaction of the real thieves would be when they found an empty vault. Gray came around sharply and broke to an immediate gallop, heading east.

————————

A FEW DAYS LATER, SHAWNEE returned to Albuquerque just after noon after leaving the bank money at the abandoned mine. He turned Gray onto Railroad Avenue from First Street and followed the streetcar track toward the area populated by hotels and related businesses. As he rode past one of the hotels, he saw that same woman, the tall one in the burgundy dress, walking into the building. Was that Randi? Surely looked like her.

Shawnee intended to settle this question once and for all. As he pulled Gray up, gunfire erupted up the street. He glanced in that direction to see four masked men exiting the bank on the corner of Railroad Avenue and Fourth Street. They hastily mounted waiting horses as occupants spilled from inside the building. Shots were traded as the masked men went to a gallop straight up the avenue.

Seizing the opportunity, Shawnee dropped the Randi question and urged Gray after the gang. He was half a city block behind them, driving Gray hard to stay with them. One of the riders stood out in his view, having no hat and a shock of stark white hair. Riding around the crowd firing after the outlaws, he chanced, getting hit by a stray bullet, and trailed them steadily out of the town and into the outskirts.

They stayed on Railroad Avenue until they reached a factory complex. They went into open country for about a half mile and picked up the road leading to the wooden structure bridging the Rio Grande. Shawnee followed, not to catch them but to keep them in sight. The great rumbling of their horses' hooves resounded as they crossed the bridge. He pressed on and saw them break right and head for the hills to the northwest. Gray galloped over the bridge. Shawnee pulled up shortly on the other side.

Watching the gang approach the hill country, he hatched a scheme to intercept them. He urged Gray to sprint north. The horse ran hard and true, easily taking difficult paths into the hills. They skirted the route Shawnee guessed the outlaws were taking and took a southeast course to cut them off.

After several minutes of sustained riding, he approached the ridge of a canyon. A narrow passageway at the end led through to open country. He caught sight of his quarry inside the ravine, about twenty feet below his level. He pulled up quickly and watched as they approached. There was that white-haired man again. Dismounting, he unsheathed the Winchester and took up a firing position on the edge of the ridge. He levered a round into the chamber and waited.

They came on fast, the white-haired man in the lead, and fell into a single-file pattern to navigate the passage ahead of them. Shawnee fired a shot that kicked up dust in front of the lead rider. Another shot followed, striking the same spot. The riders pulled up, bunching together, almost colliding. Their guns came out as they looked around for the attacker's position.

"You're in my sights." Shawnee's voice was clear as it echoed through the canyon walls. "Drop your guns and toss the money away."

"You don't want to mess with us," the white-haired man said loudly. His voice was higher than seemed appropriate for his size.

"You're the first to go down, Whitey. Do what I tell you."

A brief discussion followed among the riders, after which they dropped their side arms.

"And the rifles," Shawnee added.

That was done.

"Now, the money."

The white-haired one lifted the sack he carried so it was completely visible. He heaved it forward to land heavily on the ground close to the spots at which the two rifle shots hit.

Shawnee held the bead he had on the white-haired man. "Ride on through and keep going."

"You'll pay for this," the white head shouted.

"Not likely. Get to riding."

They complied, threading singly through the tight passage. Shawnee watched, his rifle ready, as they cleared the channel and continued. When he was certain they were gone, he lowered the rifle hammer carefully and slipped the gun into the saddle scabbard. Remounting, he rode Gray along the ridge as it descended to the level of the canyon floor. He turned into the ravine to pick up the money, certain this would get the desired rise out of the raiders. From there, he headed east.

12

A SHORT TIME AFTER THE incident, the four bank robbers, with the white-haired man in the lead, returned to the narrow passage that led to the high-walled canyon.

"Hey, Krill," one of the riders called. "You reckon that *hombre'll* still be there?"

Krill, a very tall, slim man with a long face and piercing light blue eyes, looked over his shoulder. His skin had the pasty look of an albino, which seemed to match his hair and eyes. "Would you?"

The man did not reply as Krill led the way into the canyon floor.

As they filed back in, each scanned the walls for any sign of the intruder who just a short time earlier robbed the robbers. All was quiet as each went to the spot on the ground where his weapons rested. Warily, they dismounted, retrieved their guns, and remounted.

"Yaeger ain't going to like this," the rider with the question said to Krill. "I bet he reams you a new one."

"Shut up, asshole," Krill said as he took the lead through the channel.

The four men followed him, heading northwest into high mountain country. They rode ascending slopes and winding trails into rocky terrain for a few miles. Reaching a clear rushing stream several yards wide, they stayed on its bank as they traversed ever-rising ground.

Because of the rock-riddled embankment, they had to slow their horses to a walk to prevent missteps. Ahead, the crashing sound of a waterfall about forty feet high obliterated the clatter of the horses' hooves. The riders continued until they reached the opening between the falls and the rock face behind it. Single file, they entered the opening, hugging the stone to stay dry. As each man negotiated the tiny gap, he had to turn sharply into a cave tall enough to fit a mounted man but only wide enough for one. An opening at the far end of the cave, about an eighth of a mile in the distance, allowed daylight to be seen. With light streaming in to allow limited sight, they kept going until they reached the end. There, they emerged into a vast valley that existed naturally within the mountain.

Enclosed on all sides by mountainous deposits, the depression was completely shut off from the outside world. Dense forests ringed the area. The course of the stream running off from higher elevations followed the surface that led it to the falls, constantly engulfing the valley in the sound of rushing water. It was a lush place, full of grass greener than most in the region. Randomly placed small log cabins dotted a mile-square area.

In the center of the locale, a larger building, more of a house than a cabin, faced the cave opening. It was unpainted and built with logs to a one-story height. Tree stumps on the ridge nearby indicated the source of the construction material. The door was in the center, and shutters covered window openings on each side. One shutter was open.

Krill led the men directly toward that building. As they drew rein in front, the door opened, and a medium-tall man with a slim build and reddish sandy-colored hair stepped out. He had a puffy, freckled face with tiny light blue eyes and a mouth that pursed as if in a constant state of aversion. Dressed in striped suit pants and a collarless white shirt, he spread his feet apart and poised his hands on his hips. "Mister Krill, you're not smiling." His deep voice was intense but low-key, and the words were spoken in an ominous, measured monotone. "Tell me what happened."

Krill squirmed noticeably in his saddle. "I... eh... we got waylaid."

"Waylaid," the man said with interest. He hesitated a moment. "The waylayers got waylaid." He said that slowly, raising an eyebrow, almost as if verifying he had it right.

"Well, yeah," Krill said nervously. "That's about it."

"No, it's not. Specifics, please." The man's voice remained even, but its threat was evident.

Krill hesitated, unsure how to word this.

"Mister Krill?"

Krill shifted his seat in the saddle and fidgeted. "That ranny must've followed us from the bank. Threw down on us when we got into that canyon north of Alburkurk with the narrow pass-through. He made us toss our guns and the money as well. Then he chased us off."

"And you just let him do it."

"Look, Yaeger, whoever this *hombre* is, he's smart. He outfoxed us. Trapped us so's we couldn't get to cover and couldn't fight back. We had no choice. He'd a shot us down from his perch on the ridge and took the money anyhow. Then where'd we be?"

"Why, you'd be dead, Mister Krill. That actually might not be a bad idea for all the good you're doing me right now." A wisp of a smile crossed Yaeger's face.

Krill leaned forward in his saddle. "Now, look, I told you. We didn't have no choice."

"There are *always* choices, damn it. Did you at least get a look at this... *hombre*?"

Krill leaned back a little. "Naw, he stayed hid the whole time. Why?"

Yaeger took a step forward, resuming the same posture. "Because, Mister Krill, I suspect this is the same son of a bitch who's been chipping away at us for the last few weeks. If we knew what he looks like, he'd be easier to find. But, make no mistake, find him you will." Yaeger looked away for a second, thinking, but he saw the cat dash behind a small wooden box. "You're right. He *did* outfox you. Now it's time to outfox him. See to your horse, Mister Krill, and then join me back here. We have plans to make."

When the men left to begin their preparations, Yaeger crept over to the box. He pounced, but the cat was gone. Yaeger looked all around to find the cat. There was no other place where it could have disappeared to.

"Sir?"

Yaeger looked up. Krill was standing in the doorway.

"There was a cat in here. Have you seen it?"

"I... haven't seen any cat, sir."

"It's here... somewhere."

BACK IN VALENCIA, IN ANOTHER attempt to upset the gang's operations, Shawnee tried to put out of his mind the question of Randi and why he spotted her twice in Albuquerque. Although it ate at him, he fought to stay focused on the job at hand. He almost lazily rode the main street slowly, pulling up at a saloon hitch rail where several trail-weary horses were tethered. Maybe their owners were the men he sought.

Dismounting, he glanced around, taking in several places of interest to a law breaker, a bank down the street, a Wells Fargo express office straight across, and a jeweler in the opposite direction. He guessed at the possibility of something brewing.

He wanted a look at the saloon customers to decide this. He stepped inside. The place was sparse, just a bar the length of the right side, an open area in the center, and a group of round tables with four chairs to each on the left. Only a few patrons stood at the bar while four dust-covered men in trail clothes occupied a table.

Shawnee scrutinized the ones standing and gauged them as barflies of no importance. The others sat grouped tightly together. They seemed tense as if waiting for or expecting something. There were drinks in front of them, but they did not drink or talk. They just waited.

Slowly, Shawnee moved to the near end of the bar. The barkeep reacted quickly, asking his pleasure. "Whiskey," he said. Shawnee dropped a coin on the bar in payment as the bartender poured the drink. Shawnee continued watching the men of interest.

Moments passed. Shawnee sipped at the liquor. Awful stuff it was, sharp as a knife. A gunshot sounded on the street outside as he placed the glass on the bar. Then another, coupled with shouts and unintelligible words. The four seated men sprang to their feet at the same time and bounded out the door, guns drawn.

Shawnee waited one second and headed for the door. More gunfire came as he cleared the doorway. The four from the saloon stopped in the middle of the street.

A fifth man exited the express office. He raced across the street toward the four standing there. Passing them, he swung onto a horse at the rail where Gray stood. As he turned his horse and headed up the street, two men came out of the express office, firing after him. The four in the street opened fire on them, hitting one and forcing the other back inside.

The four hurried to their horses, mounted, and went to a gallop behind the fifth. From inside the express office, the man who was driven back peeked out and emptied his revolver after the outlaws.

Shawnee moved quickly across the street to where the wounded townsman fell and took a knee to check for life. Dead. Quickly, he was up and running to Gray's side. Scooping up the reins, he swung as Gray turned and took off after the thieves.

As they cleared the town limits, Shawnee kept them in sight while searching ahead for a place to head them off. Going for all they were worth, the fleeing riders' route was open, presenting no means for Shawnee to skirt around them without being seen. His only option was to follow, hoping they would enter some rocks or trees where he could intercept them. He held Gray at a steady pace to maintain the distance behind them.

They turned toward a stand of pine trees, making straight for the dense area. Shawnee urged Gray to a greater speed as they entered and were swallowed up by the growth. He entered the woods and was forced to pull Gray back to avoid colliding with trees grown too close together to allow quick navigation.

Mounted, Krill appeared first, coming out before Shawnee from a tight overgrowth. Others followed on all four sides, effectively surrounding Shawnee. He looked around to see their side arms out and ready. He pulled up sharply.

Expecting this, almost hoping for it, Shawnee was still surprised by its fast execution. If he hadn't already looked surprised, he would have needed to feign it to convince his captors he was caught unaware.

Krill closed in, leveling his revolver on Shawnee. "Lift 'em."

Shawnee raised his hands to shoulder level as Krill reached him and took his side arm. He tossed the gun to one of the others nearby and next removed the Winchester from Shawnee's saddle holster. He threw that to another of his party.

Shawnee studied Krill, recognizing him from the canyon incident. "What's this all about?"

"You don't ask questions. You answer them," Krill said through a growl. "You're coming with us."

Thinking he shouldn't cooperate too easily, Shawnee moved toward Krill. From behind him, something struck his head. It was a glancing blow, cushioned by his hat, but enough to disorient him and cause pain. Attempting to avoid a more serious beating, he allowed himself to slump forward across Gray's neck. He pretended to lose consciousness.

"Put the hood on him and bring him along," Shawnee heard Krill say. He felt rough handling as his hands were tied, his hat was pushed back, and something came down over his head. Gray moved forward. Shawnee opened his eyes to blackness. A slight bit of light filtered through the gauzy material covering his head, but not enough for him to make anything out. Still somewhat dizzy and hurting, he forced himself to focus, to make mental notes of the progress of this occurrence. He allowed himself to be taken in tow, expecting his next stop to be the gang's hideout. At least, that was his hope.

―――――――――

OVER TIME SHAWNEE COULD NOT gauge, Gray was led through difficult country. Shawnee guessed this based on the gyrations Gray went through. As the group moved forward, he heard a conversation.

"How hard did you hit him, Steve?" Krill asked. "He should ought to come around by now."

"Weren't that hard," Steve replied.

"Hope he ain't kilt," Krill said. "Boss said he wants him alive."

"He's breathing."

A short time later, Shawnee heard the sound of rushing water, a stream, maybe, which persisted for the rest of the trip. A thought occurred to him. He had no idea where he was being taken. He would have to depend on Gray to find his way out and back again, provided they lived through this part.

The sound of the water increased in volume to the point that it seemed right beside him. He passed close by it, and droplets pelted him. They entered some sort of enclosure. As the sound faded, he got the sense of exiting the enclosure back into the open air as light shone through the black hood again. Gray moved another short distance and halted.

Movement and sounds around him told Shawnee his captors had dismounted. Hands shook him vigorously. "Wake up," Krill shouted in his ear. The volume and proximity of the voice worsened the dull ache in his head. Rough handling twisted his bonds loose and pulled him from the saddle. Several hands stood him on shaky limbs.

"Leave the hood on," a different voice said quietly. "Bring him inside."

Shawnee strained in vain to see through the hood as they shoved him forward. He stumbled slightly, managed to regain his footing, and moved as directed. The sounds of boots on wood and the dulling of light coming through the hood suggested he entered an enclosure. A room or maybe a cabin, he guessed.

"Sit him down," the unfamiliar voice said.

Hands gripped him and sat him roughly on a chair as the hood was ripped from his head. Light flooded into his eyes, momentarily blinding him. He blinked instinctively to focus on the form in front of him. Slowly, the view cleared. A sandy-haired man stood with his hands on his hips. The man's light eyes stared intensely.

"I'm going to ask you some questions," Yaeger said evenly. "Be very careful how you answer because that will determine whether you live or die."

Shawnee shrugged. "Looks like you're holding the cards, friend."

Yaeger leaned forward, his brow furrowed. "Do you think this is some kind of joke?"

Shawnee shook his head. "Not with all these hardcases around. What do you want to know?"

"I want to know why you think you can get away with disrupting my operation."

"What operation?" Shawnee couldn't make this too easy. "I don't know what the hell you're talking about."

"Do you deny you've been pulling jobs in this area, knocking over banks, lifting loot from my men?"

"Deny it? Why should I? Reckon you know what I been doing or I wouldn't be here. Sure, I'm doing them things. Everything's fair game, ain't it?"

Yaeger straightened his body and folded his arms. "No, everything is not fair game. It's my game. I decide who works this territory and who doesn't."

Shawnee shifted in the chair. "And who might you be?"

"You answer my questions. Who are you?"

"Name's Alonzo Pearce."

Krill interrupted from behind Shawnee. "I know that name." He moved forward past Shawnee and toward Yaeger. "Seen it on posters everywhere I been. He's wanted for everything, robbery, killings. Big reward on him."

Yaeger's face showed interest. "Really." His attention went back to Shawnee. "And still, you take the chances you've taken when you should be hiding out?"

Shawnee smiled a little. "Tired of hiding out. I'm trying to get a stake together so's I can head to Mexico and live high for a change."

"And you picked these parts to do it."

Shawnee shrugged. "Seemed as good as any. Easy pickings. Close enough to the border and all. Why not?"

Yaeger returned his hand to his hips. "I'll tell you why not. Because this is my operation, I run it. I say who does what here, and I will not tolerate any interference."

Shawnee shrugged again. "Well, who knew?"

That elicited anger from Yaeger. "Don't get flippant with me. I told you before that this is no joke. Whether you know it or not," His thumb and forefinger came up with a slight gap between them, "You're about this close to dying."

"I ain't being what you just said, friend. I'm dead serious. Ain't trying to horn in. Didn't even know you was here. All's I'm doing is getting my stake. Once that's done, I'm heading for the border."

Yaeger took a step forward. "If I allow it. Like I said," He again made the tight space sign. "This close."

"Been there before," Shawnee said in earnest. "Still here."

Yaeger reached into Krill's holster and extracted the man's revolver. He pointed it at Shawnee. "This close."

Shawnee gauged this *hombre* a tad *loco*, figuring this was some sort of a test. He looked Yaeger straight in the eye. "Been there before as well."

Yaeger cocked the gun.

13

SHAWNEE STUDIED YAEGER CLOSELY. "LIKE I said, you're holding the cards. Go ahead if you're a mind. Pull the trigger."

Yaeger smiled. "You've got some grit, Pearce, I'll give you that. What makes you think I won't kill you?"

"You ain't ready yet. Ain't got all your answers."

Yaeger brought the hammer forward gently to rest on the live round under it, but kept the gun trained on Shawnee. "You're right. But that does not get you off the hook. It only buys you some time. How did you plan out tripping up my men?"

"Just luck is all. Right place, right time. I read the signs and moved faster'n they done. Reckon I been doing it longer."

"He's right there," Krill chimed in. "Been on the run near ten years, I'd say."

"Closer to fifteen, truth be told," Shawnee said proudly.

"I admire your abilities, Pearce," Yaeger said. "You almost remind me of myself."

Shawnee shrugged again. "If you say so."

Yaeger, deep in thought, contorted his face. Shawnee stared at him, watching the man's wheels turn. He hoped he'd handled this correctly and guessed he would know shortly.

Yaeger replaced Krill's sidearm and turned away, deep in thought. After a few seconds, he half-turned back. "Combining our talents could benefit us both. Join me, Pearce. You'll get much more than the stake you're seeking. I'm in the process of taking over this territory. What we're doing right now is simply weakening it, throwing it into chaos. Very soon now, it will be prime for the taking, economically as well as politically. You might find your Mexico right here. You game?"

Shawnee hesitated, appearing to think the proposition over. In truth, it was exactly what he wanted, the chance to gain the leader's confidence. But he could not seem too anxious. "I ain't sure what all them big words mean, but if you're asking me to hook up with your outfit, I'll have to ponder on that."

Yaeger folded his arms. "Think fast, Pearce. One way or another, I'll get to where I'm going. If you join me, I might get there faster, but I can just as easily kill you and still get there. Your choice."

"Reckon it can't hurt none, I sign on. Sure, I'm in."

Yaeger relaxed. "Mister Krill, return his weapons and get him squared away."

Krill showed reluctance. "You sure of this?"

"Do as I tell you."

Krill made a face indicating his disagreement, but obeyed the order all the same. He reached Shawnee's revolver from his waistband and handed it over. Shawnee rose and took the weapon, holstering it.

"Give him the long gun, Steve," Krill said.

Round faced, balding Steve heaved the Winchester. Shawnee caught the gun with no effort.

Yaeger stepped in close. "Mister Krill is my second-in-command. Do what he tells you and you'll be fine."

"I hear you," Shawnee replied. "By the way, what do I call you?"

"My name's Logan Yaeger. You don't call me. I call *you.*"

Shawnee grinned and nodded, noting just how full of himself Yaeger was. Krill led the way outside the cabin. Shawnee and the group followed. Yaeger remained inside. Shawnee went to where Gray stood and slipped the Winchester in its scabbard.

He couldn't let them think he was rolling over too easy. Had to show some backbone, some orneriness.

He turned to face them. "Which one of you waddies cuffed me back there in the woods?"

"That'd be me," Steve said arrogantly.

Shawnee took one step closer to him and shot a short right jab to his face that knocked him back into the others around him. They pushed Steve back on his feet as he rubbed at the wound.

"Don't try that ever again," Shawnee said evenly. "You won't like what comes after."

Krill stepped between them, facing Shawnee. "All right, that's enough. You squared it. Now forget it. Come on with me."

Shawnee picked up Gray's reins from the ground and followed Krill. Gray moved with them.

"Leave the horse," Krill said.

"He goes where I go."

"Aw, what the hell. I don't give a shit you sleep with him."

————————————

AFTER SETTLING INTO ONE OF the four-man cabins on the property, Shawnee fed and groomed Gray in the corral just outside the main house. After about an hour, Krill approached them.

"Yaeger called a meeting," he said. "He wants you there."

Shawnee clapped the two curry brushes together, joining them by the bristles, and dropped them at Gray's hoof. He climbed over the corral fence and sided Krill for the walk.

"Just so you know," Krill said as they walked. "I'll be watching you real close. You step out of line just once and I'll see you stop breathing."

"Watch all you want. Don't bother me none."

"Hell if it bothers you or not. You just watch your step is all."

Shawnee smiled. "Sure thing."

As they approached Yaeger's house, the door opened and a stocky man in a dark suit and homburg hat came out. He mounted a waiting horse and rode toward the cave, his back to Shawnee and Krill. While Shawnee saw the man, he was unable to make out his features. He made a mental note of his general build, but the man rode off before a full view was possible. Shawnee suspected the visitor was an informant. He tried to look as if he paid no attention, but he would keep this piece of information tucked away for future reference.

He and Krill reached the house and entered. Yaeger, seated at the table in the center of the room, looked up.

"Our next job is ready for planning."

Krill sat down at the table. Shawnee took the chair he had been seated in earlier, turned it so the back faced him and straddled it.

"Where's it at?" Krill asked.

"You're going back to Albuquerque, same bank. They're moving a large gold shipment south. It will arrive at that bank tomorrow and stay overnight. They'll move it out the next morning."

"When you want we should hit it?"

"That's why I called you here. I want you to take it tomorrow night, but you'll need someone to open the vault. You'll need to kidnap the banker and force him to open it."

"That'll be tricky," Krill said. "Lot to do before nightfall. And we got to snatch the banker quiet-like."

Shawnee saw this going badly for the banker who would likely be killed once he opened the vault. Scrambling to keep his word to the governor that no one would die during his subterfuge, he quickly came up with a solution. "Got any dynamite?"

Yaeger turned to look at Shawnee. "In the tool shed. Why? What have you got in mind?"

"Break into the bank after dark. Blow the vault. That way you ain't got to worry about grabbing the banker or keeping him quiet. We'd have all night to get 'er done."

"You know about dynamite?" Krill asked.

"I know enough. Used it a time or two. Way I figure it, even if it wakes the whole town, time they cipher what's happening, we'll have the gold and be lit out of there."

Yaeger stroked his chin, showing interest in the plan. "Are you sure you can pull it off?" he asked after a moment of thought. Something moved out of the corner of his eye. Yaeger tried not to look in the direction, but his eyes darted quickly there and back.

Krill saw Yaeger's eyes move and tried to see what his boss was looking at, but there was nothing. Shawnee picked up on it as well but was more subtle. He saw nothing out of the ordinary, as well.

"I don't talk things I can't do. You interested?"

"I'm very interested. I find the shock value a blast like that will deliver to the citizens quite intriguing. I'm putting you in charge of the operation."

Krill came to his feet. "Now wait a minute here. I'm in charge."

Yaeger flashed an intense look at Krill. "Sit down, Mister Krill, and do as I say. Pearce is running this one. If it fails, it's his head on the block, not yours. You have full authority to deal with him any way you see fit."

Krill shut up and sat down.

Yaeger turned his attention back to Shawnee. "This is a big shipment, Pearce. You'll need a wagon to transport it. Assemble what you need and get it done."

Shawnee rose and turned toward the open doorway.

"Pearce," Yaeger said.

Shawnee looked around.

"I meant what I said. If this fails—"

"I heard you." Shawnee continued out the door with Krill close behind him.

Once they were out of earshot of the cabin, Shawnee asked, "Is the boss okay?"

Krill ruffled and grumbled. "Don't you be asking any damn questions about the boss."

———————

A BUCKBOARD MADE ITS WAY through the falls and onto the side of the stream. A heavy tarp covered its contents. Steve, draped in a slicker, was at the reins. Too wide to clear the opening between the falls and the cave wall, the wagon, its two-horse team and driver were pelted by the water crashing downward. Steve halted the team and beat the water from his hat. In reaction to Shawnee's having chosen him for this job, Steve shot a glaring look at him as he and Krill rode past the wagon. Two others came through the opening between the wall and the water and joined them.

"Told you to drop that beef with Steve." Krill said.

"I did," Shawnee replied.

"Then why'd you put him on the wagon, let him get drenched?"

"Thought he could handle it is all."

"From the look he just threw you, he likely reckons you still got it in for him. He'll be looking to get back at you."

"Yeah, well, he can try, he's a mind." Shawnee looked back at Steve. "Bring that wagon along."

They traveled slowly, allowing the buckboard to negotiate the rough terrain between the hideout and Albuquerque, stopping to set up a rudimentary camp on the town's outskirts. Steve proved up to the task of keeping the wagon in control, but the expression on his face was a graphic illustration of his distaste for the job and his growing hatred for Shawnee. He kept his distance from Shawnee during the time spent in the camp.

Waiting out the daylight, the group lounged near a campfire. A few played cards to pass the time. One man produced a small liquor bottle from his saddlebag and took a swig.

Shawnee caught sight of this and rose from his spot at the fire. "Put that away," he said as he approached the man. "This ain't no place for that shit. I need every man thinking sharp tonight. Do your drinking later."

The man obeyed without argument. Shawnee heard a grumble from Steve as he passed, but paid it no regard.

As night descended, Shawnee roused the group. They moved slowly into Albuquerque from the west and followed Shawnee's lead into back streets, arriving quietly and unnoticed behind the bank.

Shawnee dismounted, looking around. No guard in sight. There had to be one here somewhere. Out front, maybe. "You two," he said, indicating the two men he chose. "Get down and come with me."

They dismounted and followed Shawnee up the alley toward the street. He stopped at the entrance and stomped his foot in the dirt, making a sound loud enough to be heard for a short distance. His two companions shot looks at each other as if questioning his sanity. When footsteps sounded on the boardwalk and the guard appeared at the mouth of the alley, the reason for Shawnee's action became apparent. Shawnee grabbed the man's clothing and yanked him off balance and into the passage. Quickly, his closed fist came down on the man's jaw, knocking him out. Shawnee allowed him to slump to the ground.

"Drag him in the back," Shawnee said to one of his men. "Tie him up and gag him."

Turning to the other outlaw, he continued, "You get out there and make like you're the guard. When we blow the vault, hightail it back to us."

The man nodded and moved onto the boardwalk.

Shawnee returned to the rear of the bank as the others pulled the tarp off the bed of the buckboard. He tapped Krill on the arm and pointed to the back door of the bank. "Help me with that." They put shoulders against the door and heaved into it. Once. Again. The door crunched under the force of their bodies and swung open.

Shawnee fished a match out of his shirt pocket and struck it on his chaps. The burst of light showed the steel vault against a side wall. He found a coal oil lamp on a table and touched the match to the wick. On a low setting, it threw enough illumination for the balance of the operation to be conducted. "Bring that shit in here."

Steve and the other man carried the tool box and the dynamite sticks in from the wagon. Quickly, Shawnee assembled the big twist drill. He found a punch and a hammer in the tool kit. The punch was used to mark the spot close to the lock at which the drill bit would grind out a hole to accommodate the dynamite. Shawnee began the tedious process of twisting the drill.

Krill paced impatiently during the tense minutes it took to bore the hole.

"Quit that," Shawnee said over his shoulder.

Krill stood still, his hands locked behind his back.

Finally, Shawnee inserted the dynamite stick and lit the fuse. "Outside," he ordered. They piled through the doorway to safety outside the building and waited.

Less than a minute later, the explosion dulled their hearing as the flash lit the entire area for a split second. One man held the horses to keep them from bolting. Darkness returned. The others moved quickly back inside to find the vault door a mangled, warped jumble, hanging on by a single hinge. Shawnee struck another match to compensate for the lamp which had been obliterated by the blast. Krill, Steve, and a pudgy, sandy-haired man grabbed the two strong boxes and handfuls of loose money from inside the vault. They brought the loot outside and deposited it in the buckboard. The bills and coins were stuffed into saddlebags and heaved into the wagon.

The man posing as the guard joined them as they drew the tarp over the wagon bed and secured it in place.

Shawnee picked up Gray's reins. "All right, let's get out of here."

"Not you, Pearce," Steve growled. "You ain't going nowhere."

Shawnee turned and side-stepped in one move as Steve, ten feet away, pulled his pistol and fired a shot, narrowly missing Shawnee's side. Shawnee's gun came out quickly. His shot caught Steve squarely in the chest, knocking him back a few inches before he folded and collapsed on the ground.

"Come on," Shawnee holstered his revolver.

"You sure he's dead?" Krill mounted his horse and took a moment to adjust himself in the saddle. "Don't want him blabbing."

Shawnee mounted and pulled Gray around. "He's dead."

One of the men climbed aboard the buckboard and snapped the team up. The group rode out of the town swiftly as shouts from the street reached their ears.

14

YAEGER SPENT THE DAY LOOKING for the cat. He saw it
once and shot at it. He had to prove to the others that there
was a cat at their camp. He thought he hit it. Yaeger saw the
cat fall off the fence but when he went to retrieve the body, it was
gone and there was no blood.

He saw the cat run into the cabin. Yaeger tore into the room turning over everything to find the cat.

"Come out you, sunofabitch! I know you're here."

He looked under the bed. Nothing. He slapped his hand on the
mattress. Something soft brushed against his finger, like the fur of a—

Yaeger bolted upright and saw the tip of the cat's tail as it jumped
to the floor. He looked under the bed again and there was nothing.
Yaeger ran around to the other side. Empty.

He heard the horses in the cave.

Yaeger stepped out of the main house as Shawnee emerged from
the cave and rode into the complex, followed by Krill and the sandy haired rider. The buckboard, with the driver wearing Steve's rain
covering, exited behind them, dripping wet. Shawnee led the way to
where Yaeger stood, hands on his hips.

Faint daylight replaced darkness at the dawn hour. Yaeger looked
over the group as they stopped in front of him. "You're missing a man."

"Yeah," Krill said. "Steve had a bone to pick with Pearce. He didn't make it."

Yaeger showed concern. "If you left a man behind to talk—"

Shawnee cleared his throat. "Dead men ain't in the habit of talking."

"You'd better be certain he's dead."

"That ain't a mistake I make."

"It's your neck if you did." Yaeger relaxed, pausing for a second. "Well, did you get it?"

Shawnee gestured toward the buckboard. "Take a look."

Yaeger moved purposefully to the buckboard and released the tie holding the tarp. He threw it back and smiled broadly at the items in the bed. "It would appear, Pearce, that you do know your business. But you did lose a man."

"His choice, not mine."

Yaeger thought for a second. "I'll give you that." He looked up. "Secure this in the tool shed, then get some food and rest." Still smiling, he went back inside the house.

The group moved to the tool shed, a haphazardly built, one room wood hut that was placed at the edge of the area where the slope leading up to the surrounding ridge began. Krill dismounted and produced a key that fit the padlock securing the door. With the door open, the others dismounted and transported the loot inside. Shawnee observed the presence of spoils from many crimes stacked along the windowless wall. The other wall, with a window in the center, had tools of all sorts hanging from nails or deposited on the floor. When the work was finished, they stepped out. Krill closed and locked the door and pocketed the key.

As they returned to their horses, Krill pulled Shawnee aside. "This don't change nothing, Pearce. I'm still watching you real careful."

"I'd be surprised if you didn't."

During the next week, Shawnee took part in two more operations, an express office in Valencia and a stagecoach robbery just outside Albuquerque. He was not in charge of either job and followed Krill's direction through both. He chalked it up to luck that no injuries occurred. Satisfied with his progress in gaining Yaeger's confidence, he obeyed orders and kept to himself in his off hours.

Meanwhile, the weekend brought another visit from the man in the suit and the homburg hat. He spent just a few minutes with Yaeger inside the house and left quickly. This time, Shawnee got a look at his face. He filed the image in his memory.

Shortly after the man's departure, Yaeger called a meeting with Krill, Shawnee, and a few other members of the gang. He stood behind the table and addressed the group.

"There's another gold move in Albuquerque on Monday. Since we destroyed the bank vault, they'll use the express office this time. There is no vault in the express office, so they'll rely on guards, at least six of them, maybe more if they can get them. My plan is to hit it midday on Monday, hard, fast, and loud. Take a dozen men. Attack from all sides. Shoot up the town to distract everyone from the express office. I expect the raid to draw the guards out into the fight, so, Mister Krill, I want you, Pearce, and two men of your choice to take the gold while the town is busy. Do whatever you have to, but I want that gold, and I want the town shot to pieces. Do as much damage as you can. Once you have the gold, pull your men out. Any questions?"

"How come you're doing it in daylight?" Shawnee asked. "We can hit the express office like we hit the bank, at night, knock the guards out and get out 'fore anybody knows what's happening. That way none of our men get hurt."

"Because, Pearce, I'm beginning the next phase of this operation. It's time to take over this territory, starting with Albuquerque.

The more vulnerable it is, the easier it will be to occupy. That will be our headquarters. We'll branch out from there, Valencia, surrounding towns. Then we'll move north to Santa Fe. Within a year, New Mexico will be mine, lock, stock, and barrel. Does that answer your question?"

"Yup." Shawnee stored this information away in his memory as well. Now he needed to speed up this work before Yaeger became too powerful. He could not immediately come up with a plan. Staying with it and biding his time would have to do until something presented itself. At the same time, he found himself wishing for contact with whoever Driskill assigned to keep tabs on him, so he could report this to the marshal.

That thought shifted into something else, the whereabouts of Randi. He was sure he'd seen her twice in Albuquerque. Why was she hanging around there? Could it be she was the one Driskill sent? He let that go for the present, needing to keep his wits about him in this masquerade.

———————

ON MONDAY AFTERNOON, UNDER A bright full sun, Krill led a group of sixteen men to a grove of bushes on the side of the trail just west of Albuquerque. He called a halt. The group gathered around him.

"Pearce, Jonesy, Galindo, you're with me. We'll take the express office. The rest of you, spread out and come in from all sides. Shoot everything, whether it moves or not. Keep 'em busy and keep an eye on the express office. When you see us come out, break it off and scatter in all directions. We'll meet up back here and head for the hideout. Don't leave nobody behind to talk. If they ain't dead, get 'em out of there. Got it?"

They answered in varying volumes, satisfying Krill.

"All right, head out."

All but Shawnee and the two designees struck out in a group for the town. When they were a few yards down the trail, Krill led his group out. He held back to allow the larger force to split off and get into positions around the section in which the express office was situated, a few doors down from the corner which housed the bank.

Reaching a point just outside the street limits, Krill pulled up. His companions followed suit. "We'll wait here till the shooting starts."

Within five minutes, gunfire erupted. To Shawnee's mind, it was the equivalent of war. He hoped for as few casualties as possible, but realized there was nothing he could do to prevent violence without jeopardizing the mission.

Krill dug his spurs into his horse's flanks. "Hyaa!" The others followed, and they went to a gallop onto Railroad Avenue. As they approached the express office, several isolated gun battles took place nearby. Shawnee observed townspeople, taken by surprise, fall wounded in the street hit by shots fired from guns hidden in alleys.

As the battle raged, six men with rifles bounded into the center of the street from the express office. Confused, they bunched together, looking around, trying to understand what was happening. Two of them immediately took bullets and dropped where they stood. The other four returned fire and, too far from the safety of the express office, made for cover across the street. They hunkered down and continued to engage the hidden assailants.

Krill led his men to their objective and halted. They dismounted and handed their reins off to Galindo, a short Mexican in dirty trail clothes. He then led the horses into an alley under the cover of gunfire from raiders based in that passageway. Krill, Shawnee, and Jonesy, a tall, thin man with a black, dome crowned hat, rushed into the office.

Entering with guns drawn, they found the place empty. It was a small, one room affair with a heavy wire enclosure in one corner. The mesh extended floor to ceiling. Behind a tiny desk bearing a telegraph key, two metal boxes with padlocks securing them were stacked one on top of the other. The wire door had a lock built into it.

Krill leveled his revolver on the lock and fired twice, dulling the hearing capacity of the three men. The lock buckled and sprung the latch away. A swift push swung the door in. Shawnee joined Krill inside the cage while Jonesy kept watch on the front door.

Holstering his gun, Shawnee lifted the top box and immediately placed it back in position. "Too heavy to carry." He took a step back, drew his revolver and fired one shot at each padlock. The bullets smashed the locks. Shawnee flipped the top back and pulled out three cloth sacks.

The coins contained inside clinked as he handled them.

Quickly, Krill stepped forward and kicked the empty strongbox away to allow access to the container below it. He pulled the three sacks out as Shawnee left the cage.

Several stray bullets penetrated the front wall of the building, narrowly missing Jonesy. All three ducked. Shawnee and Krill each handed Jonesy a sack, evening the load. They waited a few seconds, rose and went to the door. Krill kicked it open. As they exited and made for the alley, Galindo appeared and gave covering fire. Quickly, they shoved the sacks into their saddlebags. All four mounted and reentered the street.

As they turned their horses to exit in the same direction they had come from, a townsman moved out from cover across the street and fired on them. Shawnee, the only one at the moment with a clear shot at the man, deliberately fired high. His shot was close enough to force the man back behind cover, but did not hit him. Krill moved into position and fired another shot that struck the barrel providing the man's cover. It was unclear to Shawnee if Krill's shot hit its mark.

"Come on," Krill shouted. "Get out of here."

All four broke into a gallop and raced up the street. They held that speed until they reached the meeting point. There, Krill called a halt.

As Shawnee pulled up beside him, Krill drew his weapon. "Don't make a move, Pearce. Nobody's that fast."

"What the hell—" Shawnee froze. This *hombre* was proving to be more than just a pain in the ass.

"That son of a bitch back there," Krill said. "He could've dropped us all. You had a clear shot at him, but you checked your aim, shot high… on purpose, looked like."

"I missed. It happens."

"You didn't miss nothing else. You didn't miss Steve."

"That's different."

"Yeah? We'll see about that. Yaeger can decide this. Jonesy, get his guns."

Jonesy moved in beside Shawnee and collected his side arm and rifle. They waited the few minutes it took for the rest of the group to gather. With Shawnee in tow, they headed for the hideout.

Dusk approached as they filed through the opening between the falls and the cave wall and through the cave. They all kept a close watch on Shawnee as Krill led the way to the main house. He dismounted and pulled Shawnee roughly out of the saddle. Shawnee stumbled and dropped to one knee. Krill grabbed his shirt and pulled him to his feet.

Yaeger stepped out of the house, studying the situation. "Mister Krill, what's all this?"

"Pearce, here, almost got some of us killed, me included. And we could've lost the gold."

Yaeger's hand went to his hips in that familiar gunfighter's pose. "Explain, please."

"Me, Pearce, Jonesy, and Galindo, we come out of the express office with the gold. We're about to head out of town when some hairpin pops up and takes a pot shot at us. Pearce had a clear shot at him, but did he drop him? No. No, siree. He shoots high—like he ain't even trying to hit him. He ain't doing us no favors being here, you ask me."

Yaeger moved to within a foot from Shawnee. "Well, Pearce, what have you got to say to that?"

Shawnee's face was expressionless. "I missed is all."

Yaeger studied him carefully for a moment. "My first inclination is to end you, but I keep getting the feeling there's more to you than meets the eye. I need to find out what that more is. Tie him up, Mister Krill, and lock him in the tool shed. Keep him there until I can figure this out."

Shawnee breathed a silent sigh of relief that he was not shot right then and there. He offered no resistance as his hands were pulled behind him and bound with rope.

Krill led the way to the tool shed. Jonesy shoved Shawnee along behind. Gray followed. The others, still mounted, rode to the shed location. There, they unloaded the sacks of gold from the saddlebags and placed them inside.

As darkness descended, Shawnee was pulled into the shed and forced to a seat on the floor. His ankles were tied. They left him there. The door was shut and locked. He heard one of the outlaws try to lead Gray away. That ended in failure as Gray whinnied and reared in defiance. Shawnee was not surprised by the horse's reaction.

"Leave the horse be," Krill said. "I don't care if he rots here."

Shawnee heard the group walk away. He made an effort to free himself but his bonds were secured too well.

Shit! Now what?

15

RAPID GUNFIRE IN THE STREETS of Albuquerque startled Randi as she descended the staircase of the Archer House, the hotel that had become her temporary headquarters. She had changed into trail clothes with the intention of making yet another horseback sweep of the region, attempting to locate the outlaws' hideout. As futile as that had been up to now, it was all she could think of to make good use of her time until Lon managed to contact her. She now made her way down to her horse which waited outside. The shots caused her to take the steps doubly quick. She bounded across the lobby to the large window that looked onto Railroad Avenue and peered out. Hotel patrons nearby scrambled for points in the lobby to use as cover.

Confusion abounded outside as townspeople scattered or returned fire toward hidden attackers on both sides of the street. The closest engagement took place several doors down from the hotel. The angle at which she viewed it afforded her a full picture. She could only guess at the extent of the battles happening out of her field of vision.

As she turned toward the door, four horsemen came down the street at a gallop. The rider closest to her was immediately recognizable through the window. The hat, chaps, and gray horse left no question in her mind. And that changed her intention from going to help people in the street to now keeping Lon in sight. This was the chance she had hoped for since beginning this vigil as Marshal Driskill's special deputy. Her assignment was to shadow Lon, but, so far, she had only caught glimpses of him. Now she had him in view, and she was not about to lose him.

She moved quickly to the door and stepped out onto the boardwalk. The sights and sounds of individual gun battles down the street from her continued. Staying close to the hotel wall, she watched as Lon and his three companions stopped at a building in the midst of the fighting and dismounted. As he and two others went inside, she watched the fourth take their horses into what appeared to be an alley. Stray bullets took chunks of wood out of the wall not six inches from her. Concerned for her own safety, she hurried to her horse, pulled the reins free and led the animal into the alleyway beside the hotel. She waited there for Lon to reappear.

Tense minutes passed. Randi held the reins tightly to keep control of her horse. From the corner of a building, she watched the chaos occurring down the street as townspeople and attackers fired at each other. Several innocent people fell wounded. Through the gun smoke, Lon and the two outlaws exited and made for the alley as the fourth man gave them cover fire. Seconds later, they appeared on the street mounted and exchanged shots with a man across the street from them. They went to a gallop and hurried out of town.

Waiting until she was confident she would not be seen by them, Randi mounted and turned her horse onto the street, following the four riders. She stayed back close to a half mile to keep them in sight, maintaining that distance until they were clear of the town limits.

As they progressed into open countryside, Randi became wary of being noticed. She dropped back a little farther and veered off the path they took. Cutting across, she entered some hilly areas that still allowed her to observe them. She reasoned they would not catch sight of her if they were not specifically looking for her.

The four men stopped outside a grove of bushes. Randi occupied a point slightly higher than their level. She reined in and pulled a telescope from her saddlebag. After adjusting the instrument, she was able to sight in on Lon as the white haired man next to him pulled a gun on him.

A chill went up her spine as she saw Lon in an untenable situation. She had no idea of the reason behind this, but she knew he was not in control. He was in danger. Her first instinct was to move in and help him. Hesitating a second, she remembered that Lon was resourceful. If she were to show her hand and upset Lon's plans now, doing so might not only wreck the entire operation but could well cost him his life. The spy glass showed a third man removing Lon's weapons. She chewed her lip nervously and waited.

Minutes later, a larger group formed around the four men. They started moving west. Randi fell in behind them, keeping to the hills and higher ground to stay out of sight while keeping them in view. She followed them in this manner for most of the day, using the scope, as they rode deeper into mountainous areas. Thankful she had traded away the skittish horse for a more seasoned animal, she had no concern about its reliability as she covered some of the roughest country she had ever encountered. This allowed her to concentrate on maintaining sight of the group and committing the route to memory.

As dusk rolled in, the outlaws, now heading northwest, followed a stream. Looking forward of the obvious course they took, Randi made out a waterfall in the distance. She continued watching them and progressed along a ridge about a quarter mile above them and a half mile back. They reached the falls and began fitting between the cascade and the mountain wall single file. Under guard, Lon rode in without resistance. Randi surmised they entered some kind of passageway behind the falls. She waited and watched.

When the last man made his way in, Randi started her mount on the treacherous descent of the slope on which she had perched. She reached level ground at the stream bed. Dismounting, she hid the horse in some bushes, tied it off and approached the falls.

With some trepidation regarding the possible presence of sentries and clueless to what lay on the other side, she checked the loads in her side arm before entering. It was now imperative that she locate Lon and ensure his safety. She took in a long breath and let it out, steeling herself against any eventuality, and stepped between the plummeting water and the rock face.

Two feet forward was an irregular opening large enough for a horse and rider to fit through. The combination of dusk and the darkness of the tunnel made it difficult to see clearly. Randi stepped in and waited, allowing her eyes to adjust to the darkness. She looked toward the end of the enclosure. Scant daylight was visible beyond the distant opening. Guessing the length of the tunnel to be in excess of forty feet, she wasted no time trying to refine that estimation. Instead, she moved on.

The walls were rough-hewn rock, the floor a combination of dirt and stone. Lifting the revolver from its holster, she held it pointing up as she advanced carefully, staying to one side. Her feet were placed carefully, tentatively. She moved slowly and quietly, suspecting that guards might be posted at the far end. The pounding her heart made was loud enough, at least to her.

She reached the opening as darkness lowered the available light even further. To be able to see past the portal without presenting a target, she pressed herself against the wall and inched forward to a position from which she could peer out. Her slow scan of the complex in the moonlight showed the placement of the many small cabins, the large house in the center, and the shed that stood alone off to the side at the start of the mountain's slope.

That tiny building held out the most interest to her because of the big gray horse standing in front of it. Even in low light, there was no question of the animal's identity. She could think of no other reason for Gray to be stationed alone at the hut. Lon must be inside.

A dry mouth accompanied her fast beating heart as Randi contemplated her next move. Her original mission, to stay available as a contact for Lon should he need one, was fast being replaced by her concern for his life. Her goal now became getting Lon out of this without any plan for what would come after that. It was obvious his amnesty would suffer, but, to her, his well-being was most important. She concentrated on the shed. Was Lon in there? Was he all right? She had to get to the hut to check on him, but there was currently too much activity to slip by without notice. The complete cessation of movement was required to allow her to safely cross the open space between her position and the building. A few inches inside the opening, with her back to the wall and her gun up and ready, she waited.

The minutes during which darkness completed its descent passed like hours for Randi. She remained in that uncomfortable position until she could be certain she could move without discovery. Most of the activity in the complex ceased. She guessed it was mealtime. Time to move.

Inching to the edge of the portal, she crouched and stayed close to the beginning of the slope leading to the ridge above. Bent over to present the least visibility, she moved slowly, carefully along the base of the incline.

Two men carrying armloads of cut firewood came down the slope a few yards in front of her. They were fully engaged in conversation as they walked. Their voices drew her attention to them. As soon as she spotted them, she stopped and dropped flat on the ground, below the level of the grass and weeds in which she moved. She pulled her hat off and held her breath, hoping their talk would continue to consume their interest. They came down the incline without awareness of what went on around them, reaching level ground and continuing toward a cabin on the far side of the complex.

Randi remained motionless until the voices faded away before she ventured a look to check her surroundings. Satisfied she was relatively safe, she rose, breathing a sigh of relief, then replaced her hat and continued on.

As she approached Gray, the horse let out a low whinny and nodded its head. Randi took that as recognition. She moved to Gray's side and came in close. "Good boy, Gray." She patted the horse's nose in greeting as well as to silence further sounds. "Stay right there," she whispered, hoping the animal understood her words.

Moving quickly to the far side of the hut, she found the window. Her efforts to see what was inside bore no success save only to assure her there was no window on the opposite side. She needed access to determine if Lon was in there. To that end, she tried the sash. It raised slightly. Encouraged, she lifted the casement to its limit. "Lon!" she said in a harsh whisper.

There was a second's pause before Lon replied in a low voice "Randi?" His voice conveyed disbelief.

"I'm coming in," she said as she raised a leg to begin the climb through the window.

"No."

Randi ignored his order. It was a tight fit, but she forced her body through the opening, grunting at the contortions required. One foot touched the floor. She pulled the trailing leg in, but her boot toe caught the window base, and she tumbled in noisily. Unhurt, she looked up from the spot where she landed and steeled herself for the possible discovery that might follow. Nothing came.

Straining her eyes in the almost nonexistent light, she made out a human form on the floor. She scrambled to her feet. "Lon, are you all right?"

"What the hell are you doing here?" He kept his voice low, but his displeasure with her presence was evident.

She moved close to him and crouched. "I followed you from Albuquerque." As her eyes adjusted, she tried to assess his current state.

"Then that was you I seen there."

"Yes, and I saw you, too, but it was too dangerous to make contact. And Driskill said to just keep an eye on you."

"Driskill sent you." It was not a question, but a verification of his suspicion.

"I talked him into it. He made me a special deputy. Look, I've got to get you out of here. You're in danger." She moved to release him from whatever bonds secured him.

"No you don't. I'm almost there. Can't quit now."

"But they could kill you." Her voice revealed her concern for him.

"Could a did that the first day, but they didn't. They ain't found me out yet. This here's a private beef with a low-hanging sidewinder, nothing more."

"It's too dangerous. I've got to—"

"I said no. I can turn this around. I got a plan. Long as you're here, you can help. Get me loose."

Realizing she was allowing her emotions to rule her decisions, Randi backed off. She felt around as he turned himself so his hands were accessible. Her fingers found the rope and fumbled to untie the knots.

"Listen close," he said as she worked. "Leader's name is Logan Yaeger. Don't mean nothing to me, but it might to Driskill and the governor. See you tell 'em that. Logan Yaeger. We got to cipher a way to draw him out in the open, out of here where he's safe. He's got a fellow, young and stocky, curly black hair, spying for him so's he's always a jump ahead of the law. We can use that against him, but we got to move on it 'fore it's too late."

Randi pulled the ropes away, and he sat up to loose the bonds on his ankles.

"I can work with Driskill on that," she said. "But how are you going to keep them from killing you?"

They got to their feet as Shawnee spoke. He shook his hands and rubbed his legs to get the blood flowing. "I ciphered a way I believe'll work. Look, from what I seen of Yaeger, it's going to take something real big to draw him out in the open, and every man-jack he's got along with him. You tell Driskill whatever he sets up's got to be a trap big enough to snare all of 'em in one loop. And tell him to let it leak out so's this spy of Yaeger's finds it out and brings him word. That's the only way he'll fall for this."

"How will I contact you when we're ready?"

"There's a high peak on the west side of the route we took to get in here from Albuquerque."

"I know the spot."

"Way I figure it, we ain't got much more'n a week 'fore Yaeger cuts this thing loose. He's loco enough to think he can take the whole territory over, and he's primed to do it real soon. Get you to riding distance of that peak and make camp. I'll sneak up there after dark and send up a smoke signal. Meet me up there when you see the smoke. Got it?"

"Yes."

"All right, now, get out of here while you still can."

Randi turned to go to the window. Emotion took her over again. She turned back and rushed to wrap her arms around Shawnee in an impromptu embrace. He pulled her in and held her close. She felt herself melt into his body, letting all other concerns go. She was where she needed to be. "I wanted you to know...." Her voice trailed off.

"I know," he whispered in her ear.

She held him tighter, burying her head in his shoulder. They remained that way for several seconds. "Lon, I—"

"Randi, you got to go."

She stepped back, realizing this was neither the time nor the place, but also not wanting to let go.

"Go!" His voice was commanding yet it showed concern.

She turned then and went to the window. "Please be careful."

He nodded. "You as well."

Fighting back tears, Randi hurried past Gray and into the tall grass, heading for the cave, her way out.

16

SHAWNEE FORCED HIMSELF THROUGH THE window opening as Randi made her way across the field between the shed and the cave. He went to the corner of the building to watch her covert movements, nervously waiting until she reached the exit.

When he was satisfied his next actions would not endanger her, he moved to Gray to greet the horse with a pat and a soft word. He picked up the grounded reins and led Gray across the distance between the hut and Yaeger's house. Although it was dark, the figures of man and horse were visible to any interested eyes, making them dead-on targets against the moonlit sky. Shawnee moved purposefully, disregarding the peril in which he placed himself. No one tried to stop him.

He reached the door to Yaeger's quarters and pounded on it loudly enough to wake the camp. Oddly, no one in the complex reacted. Within moments, a dim coal oil lamp's light shone through a nearby window. The door opened to reveal a sleepy-eyed Yaeger in a union suit and rumpled trousers, completing the adjustment of his suspenders. After a delayed reaction to the sight of Shawnee standing in the doorway, Yaeger's jaw dropped noticeably before he spoke.

"What the—How the hell did you get out?"

"Somebody left the window open," Shawnee replied nonchalantly.

"You were tied hand and foot. Krill assured me."

"I ain't give the law the slip for near fifteen years without I learned a few tricks. Ain't much or many can hold me."

Instead of giving an alarm, Yaeger engaged with Shawnee. "It would seem so."

"Reckon about now you're a mite curious why I didn't just hightail it and let you find the hut empty when you come for me."

"I am, truth be told."

"Two reasons. One, I'm right where I want to be. Two, reason I checked my aim back in Alburkurk, one of our men was right behind that *hombre*. Couldn't take the chance of hitting one of our own."

"That's not how Krill tells it."

"Krill's a blowhard. He weren't where he could see the whole picture. Made up the rest. Now, you can believe me or don't, but I'm here, I ain't gone. That should ought to count for something."

Yaeger studied Shawnee intensely for a long moment. "It actually does, Pearce," he said thoughtfully. "You could have easily slipped out and kept on going. By the time we discovered you gone, we'd never be able to catch up to you. Yet, here you are."

"You believe me?"

Yaeger nodded. "Yep. I'll show you." He reached behind the door and returned holding a revolver, but he pointed it at the floor in a non-threatening manner. Moving into the room, he pulled on boots, picked up the lamp from the table and returned to the doorway. "Step aside."

Shawnee, now curious, took a step to the side, allowing Yaeger to walk through the doorway. Yaeger moved into the center of the complex and stopped. He held the lamp waist high, illuminating himself, and raised the gun above his head. He fired one shot in the air. The resulting explosion lit the scene for a split second as the report echoed off the surrounding hills.

The entire complement of residents poured out of their cabins in various stages of undress, colliding with each other, fumbling with clothes and weapons. Drawn by the lamp's light identifying Yaeger, they collected in a group a few feet in front of him. No one noticed Shawnee or Gray standing in the shadows.

Yaeger looked over his shoulder. "Pearce. Step out."

Shawnee moved toward Yaeger. Discussion and questions began as to why they were called out. Shawnee noticed Krill and some others in the group making moves that indicated their readiness to take him down. It went no further. They remained prepared, but did not act. Shawnee stopped at Yaeger's side.

Krill ventured a question. "How'd he get loose?"

Shawnee's reply was short and sharp. "That's mine to know."

"The point is," Yaeger said. "He did get loose, but he did not run. I believe him when he says he shot high in Albuquerque because one of you was in his line of fire. He could be long gone from here. Instead he knocked on my door. He's one of us, and I accept him. You will too. Is that understood?"

The group seemed to ponder the question and did not respond.

Yaeger raised his voice. "Is that understood?"

They replied loudly.

"That's better. Now, go back to bed."

They broke up and returned to their respective quarters. Krill remained, staring at Shawnee.

Yaeger turned to Shawnee. "That should keep you from being shot in the morning. Get some sleep."

Shawnee nodded.

Yaeger continued looking at Shawnee, but spoke to Krill. "Mister Krill, let it go." He moved past Shawnee and returned to the house.

Krill stood still until Yaeger's door closed.

"I don't know what kind of bullshit you handed him," Krill said. "But I ain't buying it. I'm still watching you, real close."

Shawnee cracked a smile. "Don't surprise me none." He moved back to Gray and led the horse toward the corral.

"Real close, Pearce," Krill said after him.

———————————

THE GUNSHOT CRACKED THROUGH THE distance like a whip, sharp enough to snap her heart in two. For a second, Randi froze, her breath caught in her throat. Lon.

She shoved the thought down before it could take hold. Exiting through the tunnel and out to the creek bank, she went to her horse and mounted fast. The worry still gnawed at her—deep, sharp, constant—but she had to trust his ingenuity, his grit. He had his job. Now she had hers.

Pulling the horse around, she kicked it into motion, following the stream as fast as the terrain would allow, every stride pounding with the terror she didn't dare give voice to.

An hour of sustained riding brought her to within sight of the peak Lon had mentioned. At that point, she went east past Albuquerque and turned to the north, riding for Santa Fe with all she had.

Going day and night, with stops only to feed and water the horse, she shortened the trip to two days, riding hard into Santa Fe as dawn broke. With no place to stay, she made her way to the government corral and spent a few hours resting there while she waited for the territorial offices to open for business.

When she detected activity, she rose and straightened her clothing. She was a mess, but there was no time to remedy that now. Too much needed to be done.

She left the corral and hurried to the entrance to the Palace of the Governors. Her entry was inauspicious, but her disheveled appearance attracted the immediate attention of people in the hallways. They watched, some in surprise, some in amazement, as she walked past. She was initially embarrassed, but, as she progressed to Chief Marshal Driskill's office, she convinced herself her purpose far outweighed the need for neatness and so she carried herself proudly. Her knock on the lawman's door was answered with permission to enter.

Driskill hung his hat on a wood stanchion in the corner of the office as Randi stepped in and quickly shut the door. He looked her way. "Miss Swayze, good morning."

"Morning, Marshal," she said quickly. "I have news."

He crossed to his desk. "Come in, sit down. No disrespect, but you look like you been going for days."

Randi went to the chair in front of the desk and sat heavily. "I have because this is vital. I was just with Lon. He wants us to set up something big enough to draw the raiders out of their hideout. We have very little time to do it."

"How big?"

"As big as you can imagine. Lon said their leader is looking to take over the entire territory and he's crazy enough to do whatever it takes. He's ready to move on it soon. Whatever we come up with has to be big enough to distract him from that and important enough to pull him into the middle of it."

Driskill sat back in the chair and thought for a long moment. He shook his head. "Can't think of anything that ain't been tried before and failed. Wait a minute. You mentioned their hideout. You know where it is?"

"I do, but you can forget about trying to attack it. There's only one way in, and it only fits one man at a time. It'd be a death trap. The leader knows he's safe in there. That's why we've got to draw him out into the open."

Driskill thought some more. "I got an idea, but I ain't got the authority to pull it off."

"Who does?"

"The governor."

Randi got up. "Then we need to see the governor—now."

Driskill slapped his hands on the desk and rose. "Reckon you're running this, young lady. Let's go see the governor."

They moved quickly through the corridors to the governor's office. Driskill barged in as George Hardrick looked up, reacting to the noise.

"Governor in, George?" Driskill asked as he moved toward the door to the inner office.

Randi followed Driskill, glancing at the secretary. She compared him to Lon's description of Yaeger's spy. Could be. She also saw the silent recognition of her in his face.

Hardrick rose sharply. "Yes, but—"

"No buts," Driskill said, cutting him off. "This is important." He knocked and entered in almost one motion. Randi followed and shut the door behind her.

Wallace looked up, somewhat startled. "Chief, Miss Swayze, what is this?"

"I'll let the lady explain," Driskill said.

Randi moved forward to the desk. "I've been in touch with Lon. He's infiltrated the raiders and is at their hideout now. It's almost impenetrable. He needs us to set up something that will attract them all, the leader included, into the open so we can trap them. The leader plans to take control of New Mexico and is ready to start very soon. We have very little time to do this. The marshal has an idea, but we need your help."

Wallace leaned back. "Well, that *is* impressive. But who is the leader, exactly, and what is this idea?"

"His name is Logan Yaeger," Randi said. "Lon said either of you might know who he is. We don't."

"It sounds familiar, but I can't immediately place it. And what's the idea you have?"

"The treasury," Driskill said. "We let it slip that we're moving the treasury south to keep it safe."

Wallace looked away in deep thought. "Hmmm! That might work."

"I'm figuring we don't actually move the treasury," Driskill said. "Just move a bunch of wagons south. Hide every lawman we can scare up in them wagons and a posse a mile or so behind. Then let them owlhoots attack. What them in the wagons don't get, the posse will."

"We'll need to refine it, work on it, but I like it. It's just bold enough to convince this Yaeger he's winning. That should draw him out."

Randi interrupted. "There's something else. Yaeger has a spy bringing him information. From Lon's description of him, it could be your secretary."

"George?" Wallace was taken aback.

"It's possible."

"That might explain his absences for several days at a time. He says his mother is very ill. We'll have to proceed as if he is the spy. Leave that to me. Chief, you have full authority to make the move. Requisition whatever you need and gather your men. How long will it take to arrange?"

"Couple days, no more... seeing how we ain't *actually* moving the treasury."

Randi broke in again. "It'll take me that long to get back to Lon and let him know what we're doing."

"All right, then" Wallace said. "Get moving on it. Excellent work, Miss Swayze."

Randi smiled and nodded. She and Driskill turned for the door.

"Chief," Wallace said after them. "Whatever you need."

"Yes, sir."

As they left the governor's office, Wallace called out, "George, come in here."

———————————

ANOTHER TWO-DAY BREAKNECK RIDE SOUTH put Randi back in Albuquerque at dusk. Observing the damage that had been inflicted on the town, she renewed her determination to help take down Yaeger and his scheme of territorial conquest.

Leaving her horse at the stable, she hurried to her hotel. The building had sustained only superficial damage. None of its services was affected. She went directly to her room and washed up, then bed and a deep sleep. Before long, she was in a dream.

The river... sinking... the brownish blue-green of the water before her eyes... the arm around her waist... Lon... the closeness... coughing up water... again the closeness... then darkness... shots fired... Lon falling wounded... no, Lon, no... darkness again... awake.

Randi bolted sharply to a sitting position, short of breath, her eyes darting around the room. Damn, a dream. God, she hoped this was not a foreshadowing of events to come. Catching her breath, she lay back down and drew the covers up to her neck, suddenly cold. Lying there, she stared into the darkness, then closed her eyes. Sleep returned, a restless sleep that ended when the knock on the door announced her call to rouse.

Rising quickly, she dressed in fresh trail clothes and went for a quick breakfast. Her next stop was the nearby general store to pur-

chase food and supplies for the time she would spend in the field waiting for contact with Lon. Without the aid of a pack animal, she did
her best to secure the provisions to her own saddle. She set out to
scout a campsite within view and riding distance of the boulder peak.

Two hours out of Albuquerque, Randi arrived at the stream. The
summit was visible just off to the west. She crossed the water at a low
point to facilitate the endeavor, concentrating on remembering the
important points in camp selection she'd learned from Lon.

Randi chose higher ground that afforded the protection of boulders to the rear and a clearing to accommodate a fire. It was within
walking distance of a stream. From it, she needed a clear view of the
peak. The spot she decided upon offered all these points. She unloaded the supplies and set up. By the noon hour, she had a functioning
base with a flourishing fire. She settled in and prepared a meal of jerky
and beans. She kept the peak in sight as she ate.

She did not have to wait long. By that night, with the summit out-
lined in the light of the full moon, smoke appeared and rose in a lazy
column. With consistent precision, the pillar ceased for a few seconds, then resumed. This repeated twice before allowing the smoke
to continue uninterrupted. After a few minutes, the signal was repeated. Then the smoke column resumed.

Charged with purpose, she rose and kicked dirt over the fire to
extinguish it. She rushed to mount her still saddled horse. Going to an
immediate gallop, she headed straight toward the peak.

17

I N THE WEEK FOLLOWING RANDI'S exit from Yaeger's hideout, Shawnee took part in several raids on Albuquerque. These operations concentrated not on robbery but on destruction. Yaeger ordered full-force attacks on the town to weaken its defenses in preparation for complete occupation, phase one of his plan to assume control of the territory.

Shawnee rode with the raiders, attempting to stay in the background and avoid Krill's. Inflicting as little damage as he could became complicated in the chaos, but he succeeded without injuring anyone. He found this more exhausting than full participation in the carnage.

At the same time, random people were shot down indiscriminately, fires were set, and destruction of property ran rampant as Yaeger's men followed his instructions. Townspeople drawn out of cover to combat the blazes became open targets for the attackers. They fell in rapid succession, hit by both aimed and stray bullets.

When they returned to the hideout after the second raid, Shawnee kept to himself, taking care of Gray outside the corral. He bent over and lifted Gray's hoof between his legs, checking for embedded stones.

Krill approached. "Lost sight of you as soon as we hit town. Where'd you end up?"

Shawnee looked up from servicing the hoof. "Other end of town. Got pinned down. Had to shoot my way out." He hoped his lie would work.

"You stay with me next time out. I want you where I can see you."

Shawnee returned his attention to the hoof. "I'll do what I have to do."

Krill glared at him. "You'll do what I tell you."

Shawnee dropped Gray's hoof and straightened up, facing Krill directly. "I'll do what I have to do." His words came in an ominous, threatening tone.

Krill shoved Shawnee back against Gray's body. "You son-of-a—"

Without a word, Shawnee shot a short, straight left jab at Krill's face, catching his chin and backing him up. At the same time, with his right hand, Shawnee drew and cocked his revolver. Krill caught himself before he fell. As he straightened his body, his hand started lifting his gun out. He stopped at half draw when he saw Shawnee's piece leveled on him.

"Like you said, Krill, nobody's that fast," Shawnee growled, using Krill's own words. "Now, get this straight. I take my orders from Yaeger, not you. The sooner you savvy that, sooner we'll get along. Or we can do it the hard way. Your choice."

Krill's face scowled, showing fury. He briefly considered and then shoved the revolver back in its holster. He stared at Shawnee for another second, then turned, kicked a rock, and walked away.

Shawnee relaxed. He lowered the hammer and holstered the gun, watching Krill for a hostile move, but Krill kept walking with his head down and his shoulders slumped forward.

Krill kept his distance for the rest of the day. Still, Shawnee felt Krill's eyes on him. Shawnee went about his business, pretending not to notice.

Well into the night, after everyone had settled in and quiet prevailed, Shawnee went silently to the corral and saddled Gray. He estimated Randi had had enough time to get to Santa Fe, make the arrangements, and return to the area. It was time to move.

He led Gray through the cave and past the falls. He mounted and rode directly toward the summit where his meeting with Randi was planned. Gray's head shook as they rode, and the horse let out that low whinny. Shawnee reached to pat the horse's neck. "Good boy, Gray. I know he's back there." Shawnee's reference was to the presence of a rider following behind them. Likely Krill. Others had tried before without success. Shawnee continued riding.

The peak stood above several of the mountains in the range. Shawnee located the only trail leading to the top. It seemed remarkably well-traveled. He guessed the area had been home to the Apache, and this place, in particular, had been used as a signaling point during the Indian Wars. As he reached the summit, the moonlight was bright enough to reveal old tools and artifacts. Some tomahawks and flints had the look of Apache ownership, convincing him he was right. The haphazard abandonment of these items also told him the area was vacated, likely hurriedly, when the Army made its last attack. He had heard the stories from some who lived through that time. This scene painted a picture of the tales they told.

The flat area at the peak had been cleared of trees and bushes, likely on purpose. Unencumbered growth still surrounded the clearing. In the center, remnants of countless fires lay cold and scattered. Threadbare, partially burned, and decomposed Apache blankets lay forgotten in the dirt.

Shawnee rode in and dismounted near the tree line, grounding Gray's reins. He advanced to the site of the dead fires, likely from years past, and then looked off into the countryside, where he hoped

Randi would be waiting for his signal. He reckoned this spot was high enough to be seen from quite a distance. Figuring it would not be visible to anyone in the hideout but willing to take the chance that he might be wrong, he gathered kindling and larger branches that would fuel the fire. If he failed to go through with this because he feared being found out, all he had done and all Randi had done, to this point, would be for naught. He crouched and examined the cloth scraps in the moonlight, selecting one intact enough to work. Even if it burned completely, as long as it lasted the short time it would take to send the message, it would suffice.

Gray made that sound again, the warning whinny.

"Easy, Gray," Shawnee said as he withdrew a match from his shirt pocket. "I know." He struck the match on his pant leg and lit the kindling in several spots, fanning it gently until it caught and grew. Then, one by one, he placed branches across the flames and waited until the blaze thrived. The wood was damp enough to give off abundant smoke. With the moon silhouetting his position, he was certain the dark smoke would be easily seen against the night sky. There was no wind to interfere with the straight rise of the column. He allowed it to ascend uninterrupted for several minutes.

Laying the blanket on the ground next to the fire, he flipped it so it settled over the flames, cutting off the smoke. After several seconds, just before the blaze began catching the cloth, he pulled it back, allowing air to fuel the fire again and the smoke to rise again. He repeated this action twice more, during which the cloth smoldered. Laying the blanket flat, he stomped out the glowing embers. He repeated the entire process once more.

By now, the blanket burned in enough spots to render it useless. Shawnee discarded the cover, treading heavily over it to prevent the grass it rested on from igniting. He crouched to pull the blanket edge away from the fire. Concentrating on his work, he lost track of the threat Gray had warned about.

Gray whinnied again, but it was too late.

"I got you now, you son of a bitch," Krill said from behind him. "I knew I smelled something wrong about you."

Shawnee froze as he heard the click of the revolver cocking. Shit. He had to head this off. Now.

Squatting with his back to Krill and uncertain of how far away and exactly where Krill stood, Shawnee scraped together a crude plan of evasion to buy time.

"Who the hell are you sending sign to?" Krill asked sharply.

Shawnee said nothing. He had to distract Krill. With a swift move, he grabbed a burning branch with his gloved hand and threw it over his shoulder in Krill's general direction. At the same time, he shoved himself away from the fire and onto the charred blanket, landing on his gun arm and preventing access to his revolver. Krill fended off the fiery missile and triggered a wild shot at the spot Shawnee had occupied a split-second earlier.

Shawnee rolled on his back to free his gun arm and grabbed for the weapon. As it came out, he pulled his feet under him and pushed himself to a standing position, firing a wild shot to throw Krill off. He moved to the side immediately. Krill again fired where Shawnee had been.

Now standing with feet firmly planted, Shawnee found his bead. He fired twice. Both shots hit Krill in the center of his chest, knocking him back and dropping him to the ground close behind Gray's rear hooves. Gray shuffled forward. Krill's body twitched involuntarily, then ceased all movement.

Shawnee went forward to the fallen man to check for signs of life. He knew before he got there that Krill was dead. Two forty-four slugs dead center had a way of doing that. He rose, holstering his gun, and stomped the burning branch to extinguish it before a brush fire could start.

Leaving the fire burning as a beacon for Randi to follow, Shawnee searched the area for Krill's horse. He found it tied in some bushes farther down on the trail leading away from the summit and brought the horse back up the road, tying it off near Gray. This would be Krill's transport back to the hideout, a part of the ruse forming in Shawnee's mind to explain Krill's death and strengthen his position with Yaeger. With no certainty she was coming, he waited for Randi to arrive.

Within fifteen minutes, Shawnee heard the sound of a horse's hooves on the trail below. Gray whinnied and nodded, not the ominous warning but indicating a more contented mood. Seconds later, Randi appeared in the clearing and drew rein. Her revolver was drawn and ready.

"Randi."

"Lon." Her one-word greeting indicated her concern as she observed the scene before her.

"It's all right," Shawnee said. "He won't cause no more trouble."

She dismounted and holstered her weapon. Hurrying to him, she gave the body on the ground a sideways glance.

"I heard shots," she said. "What happened?"

"He followed me up here. Reckon he was looking to turn me in to Yaeger as a spy. Wasn't fast enough."

"Who is... was he?"

"*Hombre* name a Krill. Yaeger's top hand."

The concerned expression on her face deepened. "Did you have to kill him?"

"Didn't leave me much choice. 'Sides, he's still alive, you'd a wound up taking him to the law. Saved you the trouble."

"I would have done that willingly, but I suppose you did what you had to. I'm glad you're all right."

He smiled. "Me too. Now, did you manage to set something up with Driskill?"

"Yes. They're moving the treasury."

"What?" Shawnee, unschooled in government terminology, was confused by the word.

Randi explained. "The territory's money is kept in gold bullion in Santa Fe. They're pretending to move it to a small town down here to protect it. Instead of gold, the wagons will be filled with armed men. The plan is to take the raiders by surprise when they attack. Driskill will also have a posse following the wagons. They'll hit the raiders from behind to box them in."

"Hope that works."

"I hope so, too. I can't wait to get you out of this. It's getting way too dangerous.

"Ain't no more dangerous than I expected. Reckon it's just you being more concerned."

"You're probably right."

Shawnee turned away to address the matter of Krill's body. "Right now, I need to get Krill back to the hideout. He's my alibi. He's a spy I caught sending a smoke signal."

"Do you think they'll fall for that?"

"Don't see why not. Krill ain't in no shape to call me on it."

"Is there anything I can do to help?"

"Reckon you've done all you can," Shawnee said as he walked over to Krill's body. "You should head on back to Santa Fe. You'll be safe there."

Randi moved toward him. "You keep your head down, you hear?"

"Oh, I'm planning on it, don't worry." He said it without turning. "Go on now, get out of here."

18

THE MOON SANK BEHIND THE mountains, making way for the approaching dawn. Shawnee rode Gray and led Krill's horse, with Krill's body slung across the saddle, along the stream bank toward the falls. As he reached the entrance to the cave, the sky gave off a purplish tint that joined with the gold of the rising sun. Passing between the falls and the rock face, he entered the dark cavern and fixed his eyes on the dim daylight at the far end. He depended on Gray's confident hoof placement to navigate through.

As he emerged from the tunnel, he noted the complex was still at rest. These *hombres* were not like ranch hands, up at dawn. They only rousted once they were called out by Yaeger or, until now, Krill, and even then, they were not ready to go. Their drinking habits prevented that.

Shawnee directed Gray and Krill's mount to a centrally located water trough for a much-needed drink. He dismounted wearily and splashed water in his face to allay his exhaustion.

It had been a long, sleepless night for him and would likely continue into the day, but he could not stop thinking about Randi and their increasing closeness. If this were another time, he would have avoided involvement, as he had done with Meelee and Chrissie. In truth, he would have run from it. But this was now. Amnesty was almost in his grasp. That made having a safe life with Randi a real possibility. He had to make it to the end of this. He had to make it work.

Shawnee led both horses to the corral. At the gate, he pulled Krill's body from the saddle and let it fall to the ground, face up. Then he led the animals into the corral and unsaddled them, resting the saddles on the corral fence. Returning to the body, he leaned against the fence and waited for the camp to come to life.

The wait was short-lived. Within fifteen minutes, Jonesy and Galindo exited their cabin, and the other two occupants followed them. All four started toward the cook shack and the smell of bacon and eggs. As they walked and yawned out their leftover sleepiness, they noticed the unusual sight of Shawnee resting against the corral with a body at his feet.

Jonesy spoke first. "Hey, what the hell—" His hand pushed his hat back and scratched at his forehead.

Galindo and the other two had now become aware. The four men turned and moved in Shawnee's direction. Exiting their cabins, others were drawn to the unusual sight and joined them. They approached in a group and crowded around the scene.

"That's... that's Krill," Jonesy said in his deep, booming voice. "How'd he get dead?"

"I shot him," Shawnee said evenly.

The gathering was fraught with discussion. Several participants asked questions about the reason for Krill's death, but Shawnee said nothing in reply.

Galindo stepped forward to face Shawnee. "Hey, *amigo*, you tell us, or maybe we take you apart a little, eh?"

A few more people in the group agreed with Galindo. They moved to join him.

"I'll talk to Yaeger."

"Talk to me about *what?*" Yaeger's voice drowned the cowboy's clamoring as he strode toward the assembly. He pushed through the collected bodies and got his first glimpse of Shawnee and the corpse. He stopped short. "What the hell—" Studying Krill's body for a second, he turned his attention to Shawnee. "Are you responsible for this?"

"In a way, I reckon," Shawnee replied. "More'n likely, he is." He gestured with a hand to Krill's lifeless form.

Yaeger's hands went to his hips. "Explain."

"He drew on me."

"I said explain. Details." Yaeger's voice went up an octave.

"Couldn't sleep last night, so I come out and walked around a mite. Spotted Krill saddling up. He left, so I followed him. He went about two, maybe three miles down the river and up to a high peak. Builds a fire and starts sending up smoke signals. I called him on it. He pulled a gun. I shot back. He didn't last long enough to answer what he was doing. The way I cipher it, he's a plant, and he's signaling them. He's working for the law, maybe."

Yaeger chewed on that for a few moments. "I find it hard to believe Mister Krill was a spy."

"Believe what you want. I know what I seen."

"And he, being dead, can't refute it."

Shawnee kept his face as still as he could. "Come again?"

"He can't tell us what he was doing."

Yaeger drew his lower lip under his teeth, deep in thought. "Some of you bury Mister Krill. Pearce, you stay handy. I'll talk to you later."

Shawnee shrugged.

After a quiet discussion, four men stepped out and went to Krill's body. They lifted it and carried it toward the tool shed.

"The rest of you get breakfast," Yaeger said. "There's work to be done around here." He turned as he finished speaking and went back to the house.

Shawnee continued to lean against the corral fence.

———————

AT MID-MORNING, IN THE CORRAL, Shawnee worked brushes across Gray's back. Yaeger approached and stopped at the corral fence.

"I admire the amount of care you lavish on that animal," Yaeger said.

"Reckon I owe him that," Shawnee replied without turning. "He takes mighty good care of me."

"Tell me something, Mister Pearce. What made you follow Mister Krill last night?"

Shawnee again spoke without interrupting his work. "I wanted to know why'd he sneak out in the middle of the night like that. He'd been on me since I got here. Never could figure out why 'cepting maybe there's more to it. Got my curious up is all."

Yaeger repositioned himself at the fence. "Well, it looks like I owe you a vote of thanks here and a vote of confidence."

Shawnee stopped and turned to face Yaeger, interested. "How's that?"

"I need to fill Mister Krill's position. It's yours if you want it."

Shawnee thought for a second. "Works for me."

Yaeger nodded. "I'll call you when I need you." He walked away.

"I'll be around." Shawnee returned to the brushing, satisfied that this was working in his favor.

———————

TOWARD THE NOON HOUR, GEORGE Hardrick emerged from

the cave and directed his mount to Yaeger's house. He dismounted, grounded the reins, and went to the door.

Outside his cabin, Shawnee cleaned his revolver. This was downtime. His hat, gun belt, spurs, and chaps were still inside. He noted how seldom he felt relaxed enough to leave these items out of reach.

As he worked, he observed Hardrick's arrival. Aware that this was the informant and that he was likely here to inform Yaeger of the treasury move, he decided to hear this. He put the gun on the ground next to the cleaning supplies and headed toward the rear of Yaeger's building, tugging at his pants as if heeding the call of nature. After ensuring no one was around, he tried a back window and found it unlocked, giving him access. Amazing how trusting Yaeger was to leave his windows unlocked. Must have felt safe here. Shawnee raised the window and climbed in.

This was likely Yaeger's bedroom, judging from the furniture, chest of drawers, bed, and easy chair. Shawnee moved carefully to the door. He could hear muffled voices in the next room. Opening the door slightly allowed him to hear the conversation.

"...moving the entire treasury to Pounder Creek," Hardrick said, "south of Valencia."

"Hmm. I know where Pounder Creek is. What else do you know about all this?"

"They're already about halfway there. They're using covered wagons with just a few guards, trying to make it inconspicuous, like it's just an ordinary freight shipment. Should be easy to take."

Shawnee smiled as he heard this. The plan was working.

"If it's not a trap," Yaeger said. "They've tried this before."

"I don't think it is. Wallace sounded panicky. He's afraid he's losing control of Santa Fe and the whole government. But, think of it, Logan, the entire treasury of New Mexico. We can bankrupt the territory in one operation. It'll be easy to take over from there."

"It almost sounds too easy," Yaeger said, tamping down his excitement. As he spoke, his voice came from a spot closer to the door. The floor boards out there creaked.

Shawnee reacted to the sound by pulling closer to the wall.

"They're all desperate, Logan. Driskill's using a woman as a deputy. He probably can't get enough men to back him up."

"A woman?"

"Yes, can you believe it? She showed up pretending to be a newspaper reporter and had a meeting with Wallace. Then she was with Driskill when he came to discuss the treasury move with the governor."

Again, Shawnee smiled. This wouldn't have worked without Randi.

"Well, that is a new wrinkle. Maybe it has to do with the fact that I discovered Krill was a spy."

"A spy? Wait, you said 'was.' Is he—"

"Yes, Pearce killed him when he discovered it. It would seem they are desperate. George, this is timely. With that kind of money, we can hire all the men we need and make our move sooner than I expected. Do you know the route the wagons will take?"

"I do. The governor confided in me. They're taking the route that leads to Fort Stanton. Then they'll head west just north of the fort."

"And there's only one trail wagon that can travel down there. We'll take them just outside Pounder Creek when they think they're almost finished. They won't expect it there. Get on back to Santa Fe and keep a close eye on Wallace. Let me know if anything else develops."

Shawnee had heard enough. With the possibility of being discovered dominant in his mind, he crossed back to the window and climbed out. After closing the sash, he checked to make certain he was not noticed and then made his way to the front of his cabin. He picked up the revolver and went back to work cleaning it.

Hardrick exited the house and mounted. He turned his horse and rode quickly to the cave entrance, disappearing into its darkness.

Yaeger opened his front door and called out to Shawnee. "Mister Pearce, assemble everyone here in ten minutes."

Shawnee gave him a sloppy salute as an acknowledgment. He made the rounds of the complex, rousting the members with a call to meet in front of Yaeger's house immediately. Within the stated time, a crowd gathered and waited for Yaeger to address them.

Yaeger stepped out to meet them. "All right, people, this promises to be the last raid we will make. We're taking the entire territorial treasury. This will bankrupt the government. We've got them on the run. They will no longer have the means to fight us. Takeover is within our grasp."

The assembly reacted with shouts of glee. Yaeger raised a hand to quiet them before continuing.

"Now, they're moving the gold south to the area just above Fort Stanton, then turning west to Pounder Creek. Mister Pearce, take the force east from Pounder Creek and intercept the wagons near the town. They won't expect it so close to their destination. Hit them hard and fast. See that no one remains alive. Get ready to ride."

The group dispersed to assemble their equipment.

Shawnee moved closer to Yaeger. "Kind of thinking, maybe you ought to lead this one," he said.

"I put you in charge, Mister Pearce. Are you backing out?"

"Nothing like that. Just I'm new to this leading stuff. Mostly work alone. These *hombres* don't know me from a hole in the wall. They'll listen to you. Ain't so sure they'll listen to me. This is important as you say, I'd rest easier you giving the orders. Don't want nothing to screw it up."

Yaeger thought for a moment. "You might have a point, Mister

Pearce. This is vital to my plans. All right, I will lead this one. Stay close. Watch and learn."

Shawnee nodded. "Sure thing." Leaving to prepare for the ride, he smiled when he was out of Yaeger's view. He hoped it did not go sideways this close to the goal.

19

TUCKED INTO A GROVE OF tall bushes just outside the falls, Randi sat astride her horse, peering at the opening between the cascading water and the rock face.

She was doing something she was not supposed to do. The previous night, up on the summit a few miles south of her present location, Lon had specifically told her to return to the safety of Santa Fe. She recalled that she had never actually agreed to that, but her compliance was most likely assumed. Having left Lon there, she had returned to her campsite, broken camp, and, instead of heading for Santa Fe, she'd set out for the falls.

Arriving about an hour after sunrise, she located her current place of seclusion and waited. She intended to spend as much time here as it took to wait for the arrival of Yaeger's informant. Suspecting George Hardrick, the governor's secretary, she based his travel time on her trip from Santa Fe, certain he would come.

She waited until noon and was rewarded with the sight of the man in the suit and homburg hat Lon had described. He rode along the course of the stream toward the falls. Her spyglass gave her a closer look at the man. Confirmed. It was Hardrick. She watched him slip expertly between the water and the boulder. Clearly, he'd done this before.

She would let him deliver his message. That was part of the plan. Then, he was no longer needed. She checked the loads in her sidearm and waited for his exit. Her apprehension that Hardrick would slip through the law's grip was the driving force behind this stakeout. She envisioned him returning to Santa Fe, and he would simply disappear when the Yaeger gang was taken down. Her sense of justice could not allow that. It fell to her to snip that loose end. She pulled the deputy's badge from her skirt pocket and pinned it to her blouse in the appropriate spot. She was ready.

Hardrick's visit was short. He exited from behind the falls and followed the stream.

Randi gently touched her heels to her horse's flank and moved out of the bushes. "Hold it right there, Hardrick," she called over the sound of the falls as she entered the trail. "You're under arrest."

He stared at the gun she pointed at him. His face went white. He drew rein and raised his hands as she approached.

She stopped a safe distance from him. "Hold your coat open."

He complied, allowing her to see the absence of a weapon. Reaching her left hand into her saddlebag, she brought out handcuffs. Moving forward, she snapped one cuff on his wrist. "Hands behind your back." Again, he obeyed. She reached behind him and, leaning across his horse, closed the second cuff on the other wrist.

"Why are you here? What's this about?" he asked.

She knew he was playing the innocent role, but she went along with the game, anyway. "It's about making sure you get what you deserve. First, you're going to give me some answers. If you cooperate, it might go easier for you."

Hardrick gave no reply. Randi saw his breathing quicken. He wet his lips.

"Let's get on down the trail a ways," Randi said. "Too wide open here." She picked up his reins and moved to the front. From there, with Hardrick posing no threat, she led Hardrick's horse away.

They covered about two miles before Randi found a small opening in the bushes beside the trail. She led the way into the brush and stopped in a small clearing barely large enough to accommodate the two horses. She faced Hardrick.

"You're looking at some serious charges, George. I'd advise you to cooperate."

Hardrick shook his head. "I don't know what you want from me. I've done nothing."

"Come on, George. You fit the description of the man who's been delivering information to Yaeger. I can place you at his hideout, and my partner can identify you. You're going to prison for a long time."

"Who's Yaeger?"

She wondered how far he would take this. "You know exactly who he is. Now, if you tell me what I want to know and testify against him, I'll speak up for you. No guarantees, but it might get you a lighter sentence. Any way you slice it, you're caught in the middle of this. Talk or don't. It's up to you."

Hardrick looked away in thought.

Randi read that he was considering her proposal. She pushed harder. "I'm not waiting much longer, George. Make up your mind."

"All right, yes. What do you want to know?"

"For starters, tell me where Yaeger plans to hit those wagons moving the treasury."

"He plans to let them get almost all the way to Pounder Creek. He doesn't think they'll expect an attack so close to their destination."

That was what she needed for the present. "We can talk further later. Right now, we're going to meet the wagons and warn them. Just remember, if you try anything, anything at all, I will shoot you." Randi waved her revolver toward the trail. "Now, get going."

Occasionally referring to a map to verify direction, Randi drove them hard. Cutting across rough country slowed them somewhat, but according to her calculations, this route would eliminate vital time and distance.

Hardrick's horse stumbled an hour into the journey as they came upon some rocks. Recovering quickly enough to avoid falling, it stopped right there. "Hey," Hardrick called as he was almost unseated. "You got to release me. How am I supposed to control this horse with no hands?"

Randi, in the lead, dropped Hardrick's reins and moved alongside him. She fished the key from her skirt pocket and released one of the cuffs on his wrists. He pulled his hands in front of him, rubbing the freed wrist.

"Cuff yourself," she said.

He complied and picked up the reins.

"Stay in front of me," Randi said. "No tricks. Move out."

Hardrick started the horse moving and now guided it around obstacles. Randi fell in behind him, her gun out and covering him.

They rode that way for about two hours, reaching flat plains as they skirted around the small town of Pounder Creek. In the distance, they could see the tiny, winding waterway for which the village was named. Moving on, they put Pounder Creek to their backs and picked up the only well-traveled trail in the area. Randi called Hardrick to pick up speed on this uncluttered road.

Another hour of hard riding put them in sight of the two covered Conestoga wagons that made up Driskill's caravan. Drawn by oxen, they lumbered along and were easily reached within a few minutes.

As they closed in, Randi could make out Driskill on the seat of the lead wagon next to the driver. He was in trail clothes. A rifle lay across his lap. Randi directed Hardrick to the side of Driskill's wagon.

Recognition and then surprise showed on Driskill's face. "Well, Miss Swayze, where'd you find him?"

Randi smiled. "Coming out of Yaeger's hideout after he delivered our message."

"Picked the wrong side, George," Driskill said. "Thought you had more sense than that. Get anything out of him yet?"

"Only that Yaeger's planning to attack you just outside Pounder Creek. I stopped questioning him when I heard that. I wanted to warn you quickly. They're probably not that far behind us."

"We'll be ready for 'em. You keep heading east. You'll run into the posse about ten minutes back, likely less by now. Take a man to help you and see George gets up to Santa Fe and a nice, cozy cell. Then you can stay up there. Be safer for you."

"Marshal, you should know by now I signed on to see this through, just like Lon did. I'll turn George over to the posse, but I'm staying with them. I've got too much invested in this to back off now."

Driskill leaned back a little. "Well, now, reckon your mind's made up no matter what I say. My chief deputy, name of Maynard, he's leading the posse. See him. He'll get you squared away."

Randi's smile broadened. "I'll do that. Move out, George. We've got places to be."

Driskill smiled and shook his head as Randi and Hardrick rode on. He gave the signal for the wagons to move.

Randi pushed hard to reach the posse. In more than five minutes, she saw a contingent of riders approaching. Leading Hardrick, she rode straight for them.

The lead deputy, a broadly built man with a thin mustache, called a halt as Randi approached them and pulled rein. She'd met this man once in Santa Fe at the beginning of this operation. This was Maynard.

"What you got there, ma'am?" Maynard asked.

"This is George Hardrick, the governor's secretary. He's the raiders' spy. Marshal Driskill wants him taken to Santa Fe to await trial."

The deputy turned to call a man from the group. "Lee, take charge of this *hombre*. Take him back to Santa Fe and lock him up."

The designated man came forward and took the reins of Hardrick's horse from Randi.

"Watch him closely," Randi said.

Lee nodded and led his charge away.

"I'm riding with you," Randi said to Maynard. "I think getting the posse closer to the wagons is wise. It could save some lives."

The deputy nodded. "The way the Chief speaks of you, he thinks very highly of your opinion, so yes, ma'am, we'll move on up."

Randi moved in beside Maynard as the group resumed their travel faster.

———————

RIDING AT THE HEAD OF the full complement of the outlaw band, Yaeger led the way to the area just east of the Pounder Creek town limits. To his immediate rear, Shawnee, Jonesy, and Galindo kept pace.

The group approached the main road from the northwest, staying clear of the town, to a flat area full of pine trees and underbrush. The location held out an abundance of seclusion to launch the ambush. Yaeger raised his hand to signal a halt when they reached the trail. He studied the ground intently, determining that no wagons had passed recently. There was still time to pull this off.

"There's no telling how soon they'll show up," Yaeger said loudly. "Take cover on both sides of the trail. Follow my lead. Move in and put everything you've got into this." His words generated action.

The force split in two, and each man rode to his chosen point of attack. Shawnee moved into the pines and took cover behind a tree, remaining mounted. Close behind him, Jonesy and Galindo se-lected the same side of the road and positioned themselves on either side of Shawnee. Yaeger observed this, satisfied that his orders were being followed.

Yaeger rode east a short distance and hid himself in the bushes, watching for the arrival of the wagons. As the outlaws settled in to wait, Yaeger spotted a lone horseman on the trail riding at a gallop toward them. Uncertain of the rider's identity at this distance, he watched the man's approach until he could make out the features. It looked somewhat like George Hardrick. But what was he doing here? His orders were to return to Santa Fe to keep a close watch on the governor. For him to deviate from that, something must have been seriously wrong.

Yaeger scrutinized the man as he came closer, now definitely identifying him as Hardrick. Yaeger moved his horse into the center of the road, directly in Hardrick's path. He waved his hand above his head to get the rider's attention and then signaled a halt.

Hardrick, appearing agitated and breathless, pulled back hard on the reins, stopping his mount a few feet from Yaeger.

"Logan!" Hardrick said breathlessly. "We've got to get out of here. Pull your men out. *Now!*"

Yaeger moved forward to meet him, observing the rumpled, dirty condition of his clothing. "I told you to go back to Santa Fe. Why are you here?"

Trying to catch his breath, Hardrick spoke in a rushed manner. "I was stopped by that woman, the deputy marshal, when I left the hide-out. Driskill has a posse following the wagons. One of his men was taking me to Santa Fe, but I got him to take the handcuffs off so I could take a shit. Then I got into the bushes and managed to escape. I came to warn you. Logan, we have to get away from here. They know your plan."

Yaeger took this all in and contemplated for a second. "I see. And do they know where we're going to hit them?"

Hardrick nodded vigorously. "Yes."

"How do they know this, George?"

"That... that *woman*... she threatened to kill me if I didn't tell. I had to. Please, Logan, you owe me. You've got to protect me." There was fear in Hardrick's voice.

A look of displeasure crossed Yaeger's face. "Protect you? After you put us in their crosshairs? I think not. I owe you nothing, George. I've got more important matters to attend to than your safety."

Hardrick stared at Yaeger in disbelief. "Logan, you can't just abandon me like this." His manner changed abruptly to defensive belligerence. "I... I can expose you. If you don't protect me, I... I'll tell everything."

Yaeger drew his side arm as he spoke. "Yes, George, I know you will."

Panic gripped Hardrick as he saw the gun come out. He pulled at his horse's reins to try to get away. Yaeger fired point-blank at the man, hitting him squarely in the chest. Hardrick screamed as the bullet ripped into his body. The horse reared. Hardrick was pitched out of the saddle, landing heavily on the ground. As the horse scrambled for the bushes, Hardrick did not move.

Yaeger moved his horse closer to where Hardrick lay. He calmly fired a second round into the body as men spilled out onto the trail to investigate.

Shawnee, with Jonesy and Galindo close behind him, raced to the spot as Yaeger ejected the two spent shells from his revolver. Other men closed in and grouped around them. Questions abounded.

Yaeger raised his hand to quiet them. "Suffice to say he got what he deserved. Change of plans. We're hitting the wagons head-on. There's a posse trailing them, so this has to be done quickly. Kill them all and take the wagons. Follow me." He turned his horse and struck out east at a gallop. The outlaws followed, trampling Hardrick's body in the process.

They rode east a few miles, coming to the crest of a downhill grade. At the bottom of that hill, about a mile away, the wagons, small specks on the vast horizon, could be seen beginning the uphill climb.

Yaeger called a halt and summoned Jonesy. He leaned closer and whispered in his ear. "I don't trust Pearce. You and Galindo get the drop on him and keep him here. After the raid, take him back to the hideout. I'll deal with him there."

Jonesy nodded. He swung his horse around and moved beside Shawnee. He leaned in as if to tell Shawnee something. With a quick move, he pulled the gun from Shawnee's holster.

Shawnee reacted too late as his hand went to the empty holster. "What the hell—"

"Boss's orders. You stay here." Jonesy looked over to Galindo. "Hey, Galindo, side me."

"Que pasó?" Galindo moved closer as Yaeger led the main body of men down the hill.

"Boss says to hold Pearce here," Jonesy said as Galindo joined him. "So we ain't riding with them."

Galindo shrugged and moved to Shawnee's other side. *"Muy bien."*

"Let's get off the trail," Jonesy said, gesturing toward some bushes. "I'd just as leave be out of the saddle while we wait."

With no choice in the matter, Shawnee followed instructions. They moved behind the brush into a small clearing backed up by some boulders that stood about ten feet high.

"Get down," Jonesy told Shawnee.

Dismounting, Shawnee stood next to Gray. The two outlaws got down. Jonesy found a seat on a low rock and kept Shawnee covered. Galindo squatted and sifted dirt through his fingers.

"Light somewheres, Pearce," Jonesy said. "You're making me nervous, damn it."

Shawnee shrugged and moved slowly, almost nonchalantly, to a knee-high rock to sit down. Satisfied that Shawnee was where he wanted him, Jonesy settled in to watch his captive closely.

Rapid gunfire erupted in the distance.

20

HALFWAY UP THE HILL, THE oxen drawing the wagons labored to pull their loads. Driskill's eyes scanned the countryside in front of them, settling on the cloud of trail dust rising from the top of the hill. He knew what that was up there and the disadvantage at which this incline put them. As strong as oxen were, they were slow and plodding. Going uphill, they'd produce no speed and be no good in a running fight. Horses would have been better, but they would have worn out hauling the loads these wagons bore, a dozen men each. Six of one, half a dozen of the other, but they'd have to make the best of it as the raiders came on steadily.

Once the first shot was fired, they would be forced to return fire from almost a standstill. Better for aiming, but it placed his men in the untenable position of being sitting ducks, vulnerable to more maneuverable mounted attackers. This was not the way he planned it, but it was the way it panned out. He hoped the posse was not that far behind.

Driskill levered a round into his rifle. "Get ready, men," he called loudly. "Here they come."

Within moments, the approaching dust cloud revealed galloping riders with hand guns drawn and ready. They kept coming. The man in the lead fired a shot. That was likely the signal to attack. It quickly initiated multiple gunshots as the group spread out, giving the riders in the rear clearer ability to use their weapons.

Driskill shouldered the Winchester and laid the sights on the lead man. He fired the round and missed his intended target, but the bullet found its mark in a raider to the leader's immediate left. Not wasting time analyzing the shot, he fired another as the tarps on both wagons were lifted at almost the same time. Twenty-four riflemen opened fire in unison as the raiders ringed the slow moving wagons in a running attack. In rapid succession, at least five raiders fell from their saddles, either wounded or dead. The defenders continued the barrage, felling more horsemen.

Driskill continued firing until the cartridge capacity of the Winchester was exhausted. He slipped the rifle between his legs and went for his side arm. His target, the lead rider, folded into the group of attackers as they rode in a wide circle around the wagons. The man disappeared momentarily among the others. Driskill emptied his revolver, taking down others, but failing to hit the leader.

Next to Driskill on the seat, the driver attempted to keep the wagon moving while at the same time working his hand gun. A raider's bullet caught him in the chest. He slumped and pitched sideways off the seat to the ground, letting go of the reins.

Driskill grabbed the reins as they went slack. He tried to control the team, but the oxen had taken their heads. They bolted forward. Driskill dropped the reins, flipped his empty rifle into the wagon bed and followed it over the seat. The deputy next to him in the shooting line took a bullet in the shoulder and fell across the wagon bed at Driskill's feet. After checking the man and determining the wound was not life-threatening, Driskill returned to the fight. He reloaded his revolver almost without looking while he scanned the battle for the leader.

His target rode close enough to Driskill's wagon for the marshal to finally get a decent look at him. Recognition hit Driskill like a punch in the jaw. He knew that man, had seen him in the Palace of the Governors soon after being sworn in as chief marshal. The name escaped him. The face and build did not. He'd learn the name eventually. Maybe it was that Yaeger fellow Miss Swayze had mentioned, but that could wait. The important thing, the vital thing, was to capture or kill this *hombre* and break the back of this gang once and for all.

Flipping the revolver's loading gate closed, Driskill brought the gun back up as new gunfire in the distance grabbed not only his attention but that of the raiders. They scrambled for the bushes as Driskill glanced through the riflemen lining the length of the wagon to see Maynard and the posse riding at full gallop in what looked like a cavalry charge, firing rapidly. He turned his attention back to the attack leader, who was now making for a clearing at a right angle to the wagons in an obvious attempt to escape.

As the posse swarmed the area, raiders fell wounded or dead around the wagon. Others rode in all directions trying to get away. Some were unseated and overwhelmed, and they immediately surrendered. The ones who remained mounted were chased by posse members in all directions. Driskill laughed triumphantly at the sight.

As abruptly as it had started, the gunfire finally ceased. Lawmen took prisoners in tow.

Driskill rose as Maynard rode alongside the wagon, followed closely by Randi. They pulled up next to Driskill as he surveyed the scene.

"Looks like we got 'em this time, Chief," Maynard said.

"Looks like." Driskill placed one foot on the side of the wagon. "Give me your horse. I got a bead on the leader."

Maynard dismounted quickly. Driskill stepped up on the wagon wall and leaped into Maynard's empty saddle. Not the most graceful mount, but he got it done.

"Wrap things up here," Driskill called as he pulled the horse around and struck out in the same direction as the leader. His intention was to ride the man down and take him any way possible. With his quarry now in sight, Driskill rode hard just to keep up. As long as the terrain was flat with nothing to block line of sight, he stayed the course. After a couple miles, Yaeger veered left into more hilly country, obviously searching for a hiding place or cover from which to fight. Now following became more difficult.

Yaeger rounded a sharp bend bordered by high boulders. Driskill lost sight of him, but kept riding toward the bend. His instincts and experience kicked in, causing Driskill to rein in a few feet before the turn to avoid presenting a clear target. He pulled his revolver and eased the horse forward.

The trail bent around. Driskill hugged the boulder wall as closely as possible as he advanced into the turn. Surprisingly, nothing happened. Completing the bend, he drew rein.

At that instant, a bullet kicked up dirt a few inches forward of Driskill's horse accompanied by a handgun report. The horse reared in panic, throwing Driskill back and off balance. Helplessly, he pitched out of the saddle and landed hard on his right shoulder. His gun flew from his hand. Another shot took a chunk of earth out of the ground close to him. This time, the gun smoke was visible from the high rocks across the trail.

As his horse made for open spaces, Driskill scrambled behind some low rocks for cover. With no horse and no gun, he was trapped there. Pain radiated from his shoulder. He glanced at it to see the deformity the fall had caused. Likely dislocated. Shit!

AS THE SHOOTING IN THE distance increased, Shawnee settled on a plan to free himself from Jonesy and Galindo.

"Sounds like a real shootout," he said casually, maintaining a guise of innocence. "Say, you fellows hungry? I'm starving."

"Naw, I'm good," Jonesy replied.

Galindo shook his head.

"I got some jerky in my saddlebag. Mind if I get it?"

Jonesy gestured with his revolver. "Sure, why not?"

Shawnee rose and went to Gray. With his back to his captors, he reached into the saddlebag and felt around, not for jerky, but for the Colt Navy pistol, his backup piece, that he kept hidden there. It was the gun Toby Joe Hawks had given him, the gun he'd learned on. Hawks had taken him in tow when he was orphaned at sixteen years old and had schooled him in the use of firearms. This was the gun Hawks had given him when he sent him away from danger in Kansas to seek a new life in Texas. It, and Hawks's teachings, had saved his life many times. Now, it would do so yet again.

This had to be done quickly, almost in one move, for it to work. He gripped the butt and cocked the gun while it was still in the pouch, lessening the chance the click would be heard and shortening the time it would take to put the piece into action.

He remained with his back to Jonesy and Galindo as he lifted the pistol. Jonesy was the closest to him and was also the most dangerous. What Shawnee knew of Galindo was that the man was slow of mind and body. That made him less of a threat.

Shawnee brought the gun out close to his body, made a quick spin to face his captors. He fired, almost without aiming, at Jonesy. The ball caught Jonesy in the left shoulder, knocking him off the rock he sat on. He landed on the wounded shoulder and screamed out in pain.

Counting on Galindo being dumfounded by the move, Shawnee turned toward the man to see him transfixed on the sight of Jonesy pitching from his seat. A split second later, Galindo went for his holstered revolver. He only half cleared leather. Shawnee fired another round, aiming downward at the squatting man. It hit Galindo's throat and ripped through his gullet, lodging in his upper spine. He folded, making gurgling noises, and dropped on his side. His body gyrated violently for a second, then stopped moving.

Shawnee turned back to Jonesy as he rolled on his back and tried to put his gun in play. "Don't do it," Shawnee said as he approached. "You got no chance."

Jonesy heaved his weapon away. "Damn it!" he shouted in pain. His hand went to the wound in his shoulder. Blood streamed from the hole made by the slug.

Shawnee reached down and pulled his own Colt from Jonesy's waistband. Putting it in its holster and transferring the Navy to his left hand, he pulled off his bandana, wadded it and placed it on the wound. "I'll leave your horse," Shawnee said. "Get out of these parts pronto."

"Shit, you can't just leave me here. I'm hit bad."

"You're better off'n your partner there. Keep pressure on that. Get to a doc 'fore you bleed out." Before he finished speaking, Shawnee headed back to where Gray stood. He replaced the Navy Colt in the saddlebag and swung up into the saddle. In the distance, the gunfire from the battle increased. He guessed that the posse had arrived. Pulling Gray around, he went through the brush and pushed the horse to a gallop, riding down the hill toward the sounds of combat.

———————

MOUNTED AND ASSISTING WITH THE round-up of the prisoners, Randi caught sight of a lone rider racing toward the activity. Then she saw Maynard raise his sidearm, apparently thinking this was part of the attack.

"Don't shoot!" Randi shouted. "He's with us."

Maynard lowered his gun.

Shawnee galloped into the area and pulled up hard a few feet from Randi. "Randi, what the hell! Told you to head for Santa Fe."

"I needed to help," she said. "Are you all right?"

"I'm good. Where's Driskill?"

"He headed through that clearing." She pointed to the direction. "Chasing Yaeger."

Shawnee pulled Gray toward that path.

"Where are you going?" Randi called.

"Driskill. He'll need help."

"Not without me." Randi turned her horse.

With no time to argue, Shawnee put Gray into a gallop, scanning the ground to pick up Driskill's trail. Randi fell in behind, urging her horse on, attempting to match Gray's pace.

Periodically, Shawnee stopped to verify the tracks and signs he read, then continued at a gallop. At each stop, Randi tried to see what Shawnee saw on the ground, to no avail.

As they moved into hill country, the pursuit slowed as the trail became more difficult to make out. Shawnee made some educated guesses at that point, certain that Yaeger was doing everything he could to shake Driskill. Again, Randi could not make out the signs that seemed so obvious to Shawnee. She continued to keep up with him.

Farther down the trail, two pistol shots, spaced out, echoed in the distance. They kept moving toward the sound. After a few minutes of riding, their approach closer to the boulders brought them within sight of a horse, grazing idly.

"Driskill was riding that horse," Randi said emphatically.

Shawnee directed Gray toward the animal. When he finally got close enough, he grabbed the reins and led the horse back to where Randi waited.

"No sign of Driskill," Shawnee said. "You wait here."

"Not this time," she replied.

Shawnee shook his head at her obstinacy. "Then stay behind me." He advanced slowly into the bend.

She stayed close behind him.

Around the turn, Driskill's revolver lay on the ground. Shawnee pointed to it. "Might could be Driskill's." He drew his own Colt.

"Get down!" Driskill's voice sounded from the rocks ahead.

They looked ahead to see Driskill, his head above the rock that hid his body. Shawnee dismounted quickly, and Randi followed. Leaving the horses, they advanced carefully on foot toward Driskill.

A bullet pinged off the rock face dangerously close to them. The shot's report sounded in the distance a split second later. Shawnee looked up, following the noise, and spotted the smoke. He fired two shots in rapid succession. He could hear the plink of one of them striking stone in the boulders above them.

"Get in there!" he shouted, reaching back to grab Randi around the shoulder. He moved her quickly to the spot where Driskill hid. They crouched behind the cover of the boulder.

Shawnee looked back to see Gray herding the other horses out of the line of fire as Randi turned to Driskill to assess his wound.

"It's out of whack," Driskill said through pain.

Another shot from above ricocheted off the stone in front of them. Shawnee fired one shot in response. He turned back to Driskill who still gripped his arm. "I can help with that, but it'll hurt like hell."

"Anything's better'n this. Do your damndest."

"Lay down flat and relax."

Driskill complied as best he could. Shawnee moved to his side and took Driskill's arm in both hands, causing Driskill to grimace in new pain. "Randi," Shawnee said. "Keep Yaeger pinned down."

Randi moved into position at the boulder and drew her handgun. Taking aim at the spot where Yaeger's gun smoke had come from, she triggered the double-action revolver quickly.

Shawnee placed his foot against Driskill's side. "Hang on," he said. Driskill's face contorted in anguish as Shawnee pulled slowly and steadily on the arm to move the joint out and around to its proper location. Driskill screamed. Shawnee felt the spot where the joint should be and eased it back into position. This was done in the time it took Randi to empty her weapon at Yaeger's location. Driskill stopped hollering and settled down. Shawnee helped him to sit up.

"Thanks," Driskill said, out of breath. "That's some better."

"Well, you're out of it for now. Got to keep that arm still. Time to pry Yaeger loose." Shawnee turned to the boulder where Randi reloaded.

"You're *not* going after him alone," Randi said flatly. She didn't even look up.

"I ain't got time to keep eyes on you and him at the same time."

She stared at him intently. "Now is about damn time you understand something, Lon. I'm not backing off here. I've got more wrapped up in this than you know. I'm going with you, like it or not."

"Shit!" Driskill grunted. "Tiger by the tail."

Shawnee ignored the remark, still focused on Randi. He was impressed with her zeal and wanted to argue her out of this, but time was not on his side. Yaeger needed to be caught or killed for the amnesty to happen. The longer he waited, the less his chances became. He relented. "You'll be on your own."

"I know that. Not the first time."

Shawnee replaced the spent shells in his Colt with fresh loads as he spoke. "All right, head for the rocks on the other side. I'll cover you. When you get there, cover me."

Randi nodded.

Shawnee took aim on Yaeger's position. *"Go!"*

Randi sprinted across the open space of the trail to the other side and found cover in some rocks as Shawnee emptied his revolver in shielding fire. He immediately began reloading. Randi took up a concealed position and sighted on Yaeger's location, her gun ready. She waited for Shawnee to move.

Climbing over the cover boulder, Shawnee made for the far side of the target site on the run, but he needed to cover a longer distance. Randi opened rapid fire and ran empty before Shawnee reached his goal.

He didn't see the cat jump out at him, but his instincts caused him to duck. A pistol shot from above narrowly missed him. He fired several rounds on the move and dived for the rocks, landing on his belly and skidding into cover. Shawnee eyes darted around but there was no cat.

Randi pulled out the box of cartridges she had placed in her skirt pocket earlier to find only ten rounds remaining. She hastily reloaded.

Shawnee waved a hand to get her attention and pointed a finger toward Yaeger's cover spot. She waved back, acknowledging his message that she climbed toward it. He started his ascent.

Immediately, Randi fired into Yaeger's position. She watched Shawnee climb expertly up the boulders and duck behind some rocks at about the ten-foot level. Shawnee fired two more rounds and continued up. Randi climbed carefully and held her fire to conserve ammunition as she moved.

Their trajectory was angled to approach from two sides, to close and converge at Yaeger's twenty-foot level. They stayed hidden in the rocks. No further shots came from Yaeger's position.

Shawnee, able to move faster than Randi, reached just below where he estimated Yaeger to be. Randi continued to climb toward the spot.

Uncertain of Yaeger's exact location, Shawnee decided to continue to a higher elevation, circle behind, and seek out Yaeger from above.

Randi's path remained as straight as she could manage toward the objective.

Shawnee scrambled to a flat boulder above Yaeger. He moved to the edge, with Yaeger six feet below him, his horse tied off nearby. Boulders and smaller rocks surrounded Yaeger with an even plane about eight feet across the center. Yaeger knelt behind the forward rocks using them as cover to fire. He appeared to scan below for movement.

Suspecting his gun was empty, Shawnee stopped and checked it. Out. He reached around his gun belt to find the bullet loops vacant as well. Shit! This was supposed to be simple. Locate Yaeger and get the drop on him or kill him—his choice. Now, with his gun empty and Randi closing in, it got twice as complicated.

21

SHAWNEE SURVEYED THE SITUATION. AN empty gun. A six-foot drop. Not easy, but he would not get this close and fail. Everything hung on him succeeding here.

Glancing forward from his position, he saw Randi advancing from below. Shawnee needed to find out whether Yaeger would soon spot her, so he needed a diversion. He picked up a stone and threw it at Yaeger's horse. The horse jumped and made a frightened whinny when the projectile landed, catching Yaeger's attention.

Turning toward the disturbance, Yaeger momentarily abandoned watching the rocks below his position. It was now or never. Shawnee launched himself from the boulder's edge as Yaeger left his position to investigate the interruption. Shawnee was in mid-air, aimed straight at Yaeger, when Yaeger became aware and turned to meet his adversary. Dropping his gun, his hands went up to grip Shawnee as the two men almost collided.

With handfuls of Shawnee's shirt, Yaeger heaved to the side, deflecting Shawnee and slamming him to the ground on his back. The hard landing knocked the wind out of Shawnee. Yaeger stumbled but caught himself before falling.

Momentarily stunned and breathless, Shawnee fought to regain

control of his body as Yaeger moved in and pulled the gun from Shawnee's holster. Realizing this would buy him precious recovery time,
Shawnee did nothing to resist. Yaeger cocked the piece and aimed it
directly at Shawnee's chest. He pulled the trigger. The hammer made
a click as it fell on the empty chamber. Startled, he did it again, gaining
the same result. Shawnee rolled his body, trying to get up.

Yaeger flung the empty revolver away and turned to retrieve his
gun, spotting it on the ground a few feet to his left. He moved for it,
crouched, and picked it up.

Shawnee made it to his hands and knees as Yaeger stood up and
brought the revolver to bear. He advanced on Shawnee. Shawnee's
blood ran cold as he tried to rally.

A shot sounded, splitting the quiet, as a bullet hit Yaeger in the
left side, folding him almost in half. He remained standing and turned
toward the origin of the blast. Shawnee did the same.

Appearing from behind cover, Randi strode defiantly toward Yaeger, her gun leveled on him. In desperation, he cocked the revolver
painfully and brought it around on her. She fired again as she walked,
this time hitting him squarely in the upper chest. Gravely wounded,
he stumbled back a few inches. Still determined to prevail, he presented the weapon again. With that, she fired a third time, driving another slug into his chest. Yaeger hung there for a second, doubling over.
He dropped to the ground as a reflex action and fired his weapon into
the ground close to his foot.

Randi stopped cold. She seemed locked in place by what
she'd just done.

Shawnee got up with his back to Randi and leaned over to check
Yaeger's body for life signs. He knew by the blank expression on Yaeger's face that he was either dead or close to it. His finger on the man's
jugular confirmed what he suspected. Dead. He rose and turned to

Randi. She stood in the same spot and posed, her gun hand shaking. Shawnee went to her.

Her entire body shook. Her gaze was fixed on the body of the man she had just killed. Shawnee reached out and wrapped his hand around the revolver, keeping his eyes on hers. He tugged gently and found he needed to exert more force to remove the weapon from her hand. As she let it go, her eyes moved to lock on his. A tear formed in the corner of one eye and ran down her cheek. Her chin and lower lip quivered. Slowly, gently, he wrapped his arms around her in a comforting embrace. She whimpered ever so slightly and tensed in his arms. More tears came. He felt her body shudder, felt her holding back the emotion that swelled just below the surface, prompting him to hold her tighter. "It's all right," he whispered to her. "You're all right."

It was as if his words gave her permission to release. She wept quietly against his shoulder. They stood there for countless minutes until she regained some control. Then he let her go and turned her away from Yaeger's body, moving her to a seat on a nearby rock.

She cleared her throat and forced words out. "He's... dead, isn't he?" Her voice quivered. She started to turn her head toward the body.

Shawnee crouched in front of her and gently touched her cheek to return her gaze to him. "Don't look over there."

"Is he dead?" This came out more emphatically.

"Yeah... he's dead."

She looked away, away from the shooting, away from Shawnee, to stare into nothingness. Tears still ran from her eyes.

"You done what you had to do, Randi. You had no choice." He was not certain she heard his words at that point, but he kept talking all the same. "He'd a killed both of us. You had no choice."

She took in a shuddering breath. "There's always a choice. I didn't have to kill him."

"He woulda kept coming. He was that loco. I'm telling you, you had to do it."

She sighed heavily and wiped the tears from her eyes and her face. He placed his hand on her upper arm and stroked it gently. She placed her head on his shoulder, staring once more at nothing. They remained in that position for a long moment.

Randi began to calm. She raised her head and looked at Shawnee. "Are you all right?"

"Me? I just got the wind knocked out of me, is all. I'm fine."

She nodded. "I had visions of—. You know what went through my mind when I pulled that trigger? I knew you were right."

He cocked his head. "How's that?"

"What you said when I told you I wasn't a killer. You said, 'Nobody is till they are.' You were right."

He took a breath and let it out. "Look, you saved my life here. I can't never repay you for what you done, but I'm surely sorry you had to go through that."

"It was worth it to make sure you're safe."

He smiled. "You know what? I've met more than a few women in my time. Never one like you."

She smiled back, a preoccupied smile. "Thanks."

"And don't tell me you was just doing your job. I know it's more'n that."

Her smile broadened, still overshadowed by the incident. She did not reply.

Shawnee rose. "You up to moving?"

She stood up, rocking a little on shaky limbs. "I'll make it."

He placed her revolver back in its holster, moving to her side to shield her from the view of Yaeger's corpse. "That little trail there." He pointed to the narrow dirt path on which Yaeger's horse grazed.

"That should lead down to level ground. Why don't you head on down? Check on Driskill. I'll clean up here."

He put an arm around her and walked her to the pathway. "Go on now," he said softly. "I'll be there directly."

She moved away from his arm and started a slow, careful descent.

Shawnee picked up the horse's reins and turned to address the aftermath.

Wrapping the body in a saddle blanket and slinging it across the saddle consumed a few minutes. Shawnee surveyed the scene again. He saw the cat perched on a nearby rock. It was licking itself. The cat looked at him and continued to clean itself. He shook his head and after which he led the horse down the path to level ground. Randi stood in front of the rocks with Driskill, his wounded arm hanging straight at his side.

"Randi told me what happened up there," Driskill said.

"Yeah, she done real good. Time we get you back to the wagons. That shoulder needs tending." He let out a whistle and a call, "Gray, come on, boy."

Within seconds, Gray, followed by the other two horses, returned. In short order, they were mounted and heading slowly back to the attack location.

———————

IN THE FOLLOWING WEEK, SHAWNEE, accompanied by Deputy Marshal Maynard, accomplished the return of the loot he had stored at the abandoned mine. Maynard was impressed with Shawnee's record keeping of where the loot came from. The deputy marshal offered Shawnee a job on the spot. Shawnee chuckled and declined. At the same time, Randi submitted her final report and expenses to Pinkerton headquarters. She waited at a hotel in Santa Fe for Shawnee to return.

Driskill received medical treatment for the dislocated shoulder and was ordered to rest for a few days. He ignored the orders and returned to his desk to dictate his report of the Yaeger incident, a vital addition to the case against the captured gang members.

Shawnee and Maynard entered Santa Fe on horseback. When they reached Randi's hotel, Maynard took his leave to check in with Driskill for reassignment. For the first time in fifteen years, Shawnee took a room in the hotel and signed in as Alonzo Pearce without the concern of being arrested. He walked unguarded to his room and dropped his gear. When he heard a knock on the door, he opened it to find Randi in that flattering burgundy dress staring off into nothing. He smiled.

"I saw you come into the lobby." She wiped away the corners of her eyes to regain her composure. "Governor Wallace asked to see you as soon as you arrived. I'm sure it has to do with your amnesty."

"Well, I ain't all that presentable, but I can go now if'n that's all right."

"You look fine to me. Would you like some company?"

His smile broadened. "Surely would. You being part and parcel of this, you should ought to be there."

She placed her arm inside the crook of his arm. "Shall we?"

"Yes, ma'am, we shall."

They walked arm in arm from the hotel to the Palace of the Governors and straight to the governor's office. As they stepped inside, a new secretary, replacing George Hardrick, looked up from the desk. She was a pleasant-looking young woman with spectacles and mousey brown hair pulled back in a bun.

"Good day. May I help you?"

Randi cleared her throat and spoke up. "Alonzo Pearce and Randi Swayze to see the governor."

"Oh, yes. Governor Wallace is expecting you." The woman got

up and tapped on the door to the inner office. Opening the door, she peeked in. "Mister Pearce and Miss Swayze, sir."

"Yes, send them in."

The woman opened the door fully and stood aside. Shawnee and Randi stepped in.

Governor Wallace rose as they entered. He extended his hand to Shawnee. "Mister Pearce, I can't tell you how grateful I am."

Feeling a little self-conscious, Shawnee just grinned as he shook hands with the governor.

Wallace turned his attention to Randi. "And you, Miss Swayze, you are a constant source of amazement to me. You've gone well above and beyond the call of any duty you've taken on. I intend to commend you highly to Mister Pinkerton. Thank you."

Randi smiled. "You're very kind, sir."

"Please, sit down," Wallace said. He sat as they took seats, and he continued, "You might be interested in the developments of this past week. Our investigation of Yaeger and Hardrick has turned up the names of quite a few members of this government who were involved in some way in Yaeger's scheme. As an aside, we determined that Hardrick's sick mother, whom he constantly used as an excuse for his absences, is nonexistent. She died several years ago. Several suspects have already been identified as involved in the Santa Fe Ring. Indictments will be forthcoming."

Wallace's smile changed to a frown.

"Unfortunately, the ring itself is still basically intact and is powerful enough to resist any efforts I can put forth to disrupt them. Now, they've gone completely underground." The governor breathed a sigh and looked off into space. "Quite frankly, I'm at my wit's end and exhausted. I've asked the president to send a replacement for this office. Someone else can continue this fight. I plan to retire and pursue my writing. However, right now, to the business at hand."

He pushed back from his desk and reached into the top drawer. He brought out a sheet of paper, signed it at the bottom, blotted the signature, and handed the document to Shawnee. "This is your proclamation of amnesty. It is legal and within my authority as a federal officer. Therefore, it applies throughout the United States. Before I leave office, I will endeavor to destroy as many wanted posters with your name on them as we can find. However, I can only order that within this territory. If you leave New Mexico, keep that document handy. It will save you some difficulty if a wanted poster turns up on you."

Shawnee took the paper and looked it over. Wallace handed him an envelope bearing the imprint of the territorial government. Shawnee folded the page and placed it in the envelope.

"Now," Wallace said, "you are a free man if you do not break any additional laws. As I told you once before, if you do, as Billy Bonney did, you will answer for that offense. Do you understand the terms?"

"Reckon so," Shawnee replied. "I screw up, and I'm right back where I started."

"Essentially, yes."

"I give you my word, Governor, I ain't going to screw this up."

"I'm sure you won't."

They rose in unison. Wallace shook Shawnee's hand once more.

"Again," Wallace said. "More thanks than I can say."

"None needed, Governor. You said it all here." Shawnee pointed at the amnesty paper.

Wallace turned to Randi. "It's been a distinct pleasure knowing you, Miss Swayze."

"For me as well, sir."

Shawnee and Randi went to the door.

"Godspeed to you both," Wallace said after them.

They both said their thanks and left. As they exited the building, Randi stopped and turned to Shawnee.

"So, do you have any plans for the future now that you have one?"

Shawnee's hand went to the back of his neck. "Well, first off, keep my nose clean, stay out of trouble. Head west, I reckon. Somewheres I ain't knowed. California, maybe. Maybe up north. Get a job. Save up some money. Start up a little spread. Run some cattle. Learned all about that working the Tell Ranch. Reckon that'll do for starters."

She laid her hand on his arm and smiled. "Sounds like you've been thinking about that for quite a while. Have you... considered taking someone along with you, someone to keep you company?"

Lon smiled at her. "Like you, maybe?"

Randi smiled back. "Uh-huh."

He felt blood rush to his face in an uninhibited blush. "Well, now, that surely sounds like something I'd admire to do."

BOB GIEL WAS A GIFTED storyteller who brought the spirit of the Old West to life through his compelling, adventure-filled novels. A five-star reviewed author of late 19th-century Western fiction, he dedicated his later years to capturing the grit, determination, and unyielding spirit of those who lived and died on the frontier.

From a young age, Giel was captivated by the cowboy life, inspired by the B-Western heroes of the 1940s and '50s. Though he spent much of his career in the corporate world, his love for the West never faded. Upon retirement, he embraced his passion for writing, crafting ten unforgettable Western novels and embarking on an ambitious eleven-book series. His commitment to the genre earned him a place among the esteemed members of the Western Writers of America.

Born in New York and later residing in New Jersey, Giel spent his days weaving tales of honor, survival, and justice—ensuring that the legends of the frontier would never be forgotten. His stories continue to inspire readers, preserving a bygone era with every turn of the page. Though he is no longer with us, his words live on, carrying his love for the West into the hearts of those who cherish the stories he left behind.

9 7 9 8 8 9 2 9 9 0 5 6 1